ROCK HOUNDS

ROCK HOUNDS

Evelyn Sibley Lampman

ILLUSTRATED BY ARNOLD SPILKA

Doubleday & Company, Inc., Garden City, New York

Library of Congress Catalog Card Number 58-9661
Printed in the United States of America.

For Catherine McCanna,
who asked for a book
about rocks.

AUTHOR'S NOTE

Camp Hancock is a real camp, located in the Carno Basin near the town of Fossil, about 175 miles from the city of Portland, Oregon. And Mr. and Mrs. A. W. Hancock are real people, who have devoted their lives to the furthering of an interest in science in boys and girls.

I heard of them first twelve years ago, when my elder daughter was in the fourth grade, and visited the Rock Room in the Hancock home with her science class from school. She returned home greatly excited, not only about the specimens of rocks and minerals she had seen, but about the fossil display. Moreover, she understood what she had seen, for Mr. Hancock's accompanying talk, geared to her age level, had made these matters far clearer than any textbook. During the past years, over twenty thousand school children have enjoyed the same experience. There has never been any charge, and there is no way of estimating the interest or educational value instilled in our young people by these visits.

Five years ago Mr. Hancock decided to take some of the more enthusiastic young scientists with him on his summer expeditions in search of specimens. Camp Hancock is the outcome of that idea. Offers of assistance came from every hand. Instructors and professors from our colleges and universities volunteered their services as leaders in their special fields. Doctors and registered nurses heard about the project and arranged to take their own vacations at the camp so they could be on hand in case of emergencies. Financially, Camp Hancock barely breaks even each year, for the cost to campers covers only their board bill for the two weeks, a sum which most of the boys and girls work to earn for themselves. It is now under the sponsorship of the Oregon Museum of Science and Industry, and is, so far as I can discover, the only one like it in the United States. It is a dream of Mr. Hancock that a second camp may someday be opened at the seashore to supplement the one already in the desert country.

I wish to thank Mr. and Mrs. Hancock for permission to use their names in this book, and my thanks also go to Mr. Robert VanAtta, of Portland State College, director of the 1957 session, and to Beth and Richard Olson, two of the campers, for their invaluable assistance.

E.S.L.

ROCK HOUNDS

One

"It's time to leave for the airport, Eddie," called Mrs. Herrick.

Ed took one last admiring look at his prize thunderegg, the one which, when sawed open had proved to contain an almost perfect marine scene. Then he replaced it carefully on the shelf with his other specimens.

"I'm coming, Mom," he shouted. As he reached the kitchen where Mrs. Herrick was waiting, the car keys jingling from her fingers, he added reproachfully, "And please don't call me Eddie."

"I'm sorry, Ed," said his mother meekly. "It's just that you've always been Eddie."

"Eddie's okay for little kids. I'm not a little kid any more. I'm twelve."

"I know, dear. I'll try to remember."

"You'll just have to remember," he said firmly.

"It's more important than ever now. What if you should forget and call me that in front of *her?*"

"Now, now, Ed," soothed his mother, shooing him out of the door and closing it behind them. "It's not going to be so bad as you think. I'm sure your cousin Priscilla is a very nice girl. Before the summer's over, you'll be the very best of friends."

"Friends with a girl!" He snorted with disbelief. "Mom, you sure do get crazy ideas sometimes. Besides, I probably won't even see her except at meals. Saturday I go to Camp Hancock. And after that, Duane and I have lots of things to do."

"I'm sorry you must leave for camp so soon after Priscilla arrives," said Mrs. Herrick soberly. "But two weeks isn't very long, and I'm sure you and Duane wouldn't be so rude as to exclude Priscilla from everything you do when you get back."

"She wouldn't be interested in what we do," pointed out Ed. "You introduce her to some girls while I'm gone, and she can run around with them for the rest of the summer. Hey, how about letting me back the car out of the garage?"

"No," said his mother quickly, sliding under the wheel. "There's plenty of time for that when you're old enough for a license."

"Okay," shrugged Ed.

His suggestion about backing out the car had

been automatic. He had known he wouldn't be allowed to do so.

He watched critically as she maneuvered the car out of the garage and got under way. When a light changed just as they reached an intersection and his mother's hastily applied foot on the brake resulted in a slight bump, he allowed himself a superior masculine smile, but he wisely refrained from comment.

"Eddie—I mean, Ed," began his mother, once they had resumed their progress, "I wish you'd do me a favor."

"Why, sure, Mom." He looked at her affectionately, surprised at something in her tone.

"I wish you'd promise me to be nice to Priscilla while she's here."

"What do you mean, nice?"

"Just polite and friendly. After all, it isn't her fault she's a girl."

"I suppose not," he agreed reluctantly.

"And when you come right down to it, there's nothing wrong with being a girl. I'm a girl."

"You're different," he told her quickly. "Besides, you're not a girl. You're a lady."

"But I was a girl once. And girls have feelings too. I want you to remember that Priscilla will be a long way from her home this summer. It's the first time she's ever been away from her mother for any length of time, and she wouldn't be here now if

Aunt Marie hadn't been sent to Paris on business. It's going to be a little strange for Priscilla, I'm afraid."

"I don't see how you can expect me to do anything," he protested. "I'll be polite, sure. But I'm certainly not going to play dolls with her."

"Of course not," said Mrs. Herrick quickly. "And I'll see that she meets some girls her own age just as soon as possible. Perhaps we could give a little party. You and Duane could make up a list for me from boys and girls in your class at school. Since Priscilla is your age, you—"

"No, Mom," he interrupted quickly. "I don't think a party's a good idea. At least not a party with boys. They wouldn't want to come. There wouldn't be anything to do but sit and listen to the girls giggle."

Mrs. Herrick gave in with a little sigh.

"Very well," she agreed. "No party. But you will be polite, won't you, Ed? You'll remember to do that?"

"Sure, Mom," he promised grandly. "I'll be polite whenever I happen to be around. But I'm going to be pretty busy this summer. I won't be around very much."

Although he had never laid eyes on her before, Ed had no trouble identifying his cousin as soon as she stepped off the plane, and he didn't like what he saw. She was the only child on the flight, but

"She looks stuck up," he told himself grimly

she didn't seem to be intimidated by the fact. She crossed the field alone, her head held rather high—she looks stuck up, he told himself grimly—and there was an air of poise and assurance about her which he resented. After all, she didn't need to act as though an airplane trip halfway across the country were an everyday affair. She ought to look impressed, as Ed, who had never been up in a plane, would be, or scared at this first meeting with strange relatives. Instead, she looked very calm and as though she were ready to cope with any emergency.

Mrs. Herrick pushed forward as Priscilla came through the gate.

"Priscilla," she called eagerly. "Over here."

Priscilla turned and smiled. She was tall for her age, taller than he, Ed observed grudgingly, but very skinny. He doubted if she had any muscle at all, although of course he couldn't be sure under that blue coat thing she had on. She wore some kind of a hat with flowers on it that was shaped in back so that her pony tail could stick out, and the pony tail was the color of broom straws. So far as girls went he guessed she wasn't too bad-looking, and he had to admit, to her credit, that as yet she hadn't giggled. Then he noticed her hands. She was wearing gloves. Gloves! Who did she think she was, anyway? Who was she trying to impress?

"You must be Aunt Margaret," Priscilla was

saying. There was something peculiar in the way she pronounced her words. It was particularly noticeable in the way she said "aunt." Ed scowled fiercely.

"Of course I am," said Mrs. Herrick, giving her a quick hug. "Let me look at you, dear. You have your mother's eyes but your father's nose. Oh, it's so nice to have you here."

"It's nice to be here, Aunt Margaret," said Priscilla gravely. "I've been looking forward to it. All the girls at Miss Barrett's have been envying me ever since Mother told me I'd be spending my whole holiday in the Far West."

"Good," smiled Mrs. Herrick. Then she remembered Ed and pulled him forward. "This is your cousin Ed, Priscilla. I hope you two will become very good friends."

"I'm sure we will, Aunt Margaret," said Priscilla. She looked at her cousin, but under his critical stare the smile she had worn ever since she had come through the gate grew a little strained at the corners. There was an imperceptible pause, then she put out her hand. "How do you do, Edwin," she said graciously.

"Hi," said Ed. He touched the gloved hand quickly, then dropped it in panic. This was going to be even worse than he had imagined. Giggling little girls he could ignore. He was accustomed to them. But what was he expected to do about a girl his own age who pretended to be grown up and used dancing-school manners on everyday occasions?

"Do you have your claim checks, dear?" asked Mrs. Herrick, looking at Priscilla with evident approval. "We'll pick up your bags and then be on our way."

"I'll get them," said Ed quickly. "Why don't you and—and Priscilla go sit in the car?"

He had to get away from this strange and frightening girl; and, while there was no way to avoid the ride back home with her, he might be able to avoid her company during the wait for the baggage.

Mrs. Herrick regarded her son with some surprise and much pleasure. It wasn't like Eddie to be so thoughtful.

"Do you have a great deal of baggage, Priscilla? Will he be able to manage it alone?"

"Just two bags," said Priscilla. "They aren't heavy. The rest of my things were shipped."

"Then we will wait in the car," decided Mrs. Herrick. "Come as quickly as you can, Ed."

Ed waited until everyone else had claimed his luggage before he presented Priscilla's claim checks. Then he carried the two bags to the car and put them in the trunk.

"I'll sit in back," he volunteered. "No sense in squashing three in the front seat when there's plenty of room in back."

"Fine," said Mrs. Herrick gaily, turning on the ignition. She and Priscilla were getting along like two lovebirds in a cage, Ed decided. It was a good thing, too, because they'd be company for each other. He hoped they would keep it that way, but unfortunately they didn't. The girl turned around halfway in her seat and with that irritating grown-up manner of hers tried to include him in the conversation.

"Aunt Margaret's been telling me that you're going to a camp day after tomorrow."

"Yeah," said Ed, studying the landscape as they drove along.

"She says it's a special kind of camp, for people who are interested in science. I've never heard of a camp like that."

Ed nodded without saying anything, and his mother prompted him from the front seat.

"I wish you'd explain it to Priscilla, Ed. She's very interested in botany. She says it was one of her favorite subjects. They have field trips in botany at Camp Hancock, don't they?"

"Yeah, I guess so. I never went on one of them," said Ed. "I was too busy."

"Ed spent most of his time looking for rocks,"

said Mrs. Herrick quickly. "You must see his collection when we get home. He's a real rock hound."

"Rock hound?" repeated Priscilla.

"It's what they call people who are especially interested in rocks," explained Mrs. Herrick.

"Oh," said Priscilla politely, and turned to face the front.

Although Mrs. Herrick seemed entirely oblivious to the fact, Ed could tell by Priscilla's tone that she wasn't the slightest bit interested in his rock collection. Of course he hadn't really expected a girl to understand about something so important, but somehow he was now stirred to a new resentment. Okay, if that's how she felt, she'd never get to see it. People who were too dumb to appreciate such things shouldn't be allowed to see them. And she was dumb. For all her airs, she probably wouldn't know the difference between a rock and a mineral; and he, Ed, would never enlighten her either. She could just go along the rest of her life in total ignorance, and he'd contribute to that ignorance by keeping the door to the basement workroom locked.

Mrs. Herrick turned into the driveway beside their house.

"Well, here we are," she said brightly. "We're home, Priscilla."

"Really?" Priscilla looked around her eagerly. "It's such a pretty district. All these green lawns and flowers and trees. I'm going to love it here. We've always lived in an apartment, you know. The nearest grass was in the park."

"I know," said Mrs. Herrick gently, and Ed pricked up his ears in amazement. That was a funny way to live. It might account, just a little, for his cousin's strangeness.

"Everything's very different from the way I expected it to be," confided Priscilla. "I knew, of course, that the Far West wouldn't be exactly the way it is in the movies. But I did think that by this time we'd have seen at least one Indian."

Ed rolled on the seat in helpless laughter

The confession was too much for Ed. He rolled on the seat in helpless laughter.

"Indians!" he shrieked. "She actually thought she'd see Indians, maybe in feathers and war paint! Oh, brother, how dumb can you be!"

Two

Priscilla took as long as possible to transfer her belongings from the two bags into drawers and onto hangers. Aunt Margaret had asked if she'd like to rest from the plane trip, and Priscilla had said yes, not because she was tired, but because she wanted to get away from that horrid boy. If she had only known about him, she wouldn't have come in the first place. There were summer camps near home where she could have gone while Mother was away. She had vetoed that suggestion because she didn't like camps. They were too regimented, and she got enough of that in school. Summers were made for vacations, and she had foolishly thought this would be the best vacation she had ever had.

She made a face at the last articles in the second bag and hastily concealed them in the bottom of one of the drawers, beneath her underwear. They were new riding boots, and their selection had occupied one whole afternoon. They had to be exactly right, she had told herself. The sort of boots which were acceptable in Eastern riding academies might be laughed at in western Oregon.

The salesman, a gentleman who spoke with authority, assured her these were what everyone would be wearing out West; she couldn't go wrong with this pair. Perhaps he was right, but she had seen no one in riding clothes, much less a horse, since her arrival, and after her terrible blunder in mentioning Indians, she certainly wouldn't venture a question on the subject.

Her ears burned as she remembered Edwin's laughter when she had mentioned Indians. How rude he was, and unpolished. The girls at Miss Barrett's had thought it exciting that she had a boy cousin her own age, but they wouldn't think so if they could see Edwin. His black hair was in need of cutting, and someone should tell him to keep the tail of his tee shirt tucked inside his jeans. And those awful tennis shoes he wore!

But even worse than his physical appearance were his manners. She couldn't imagine anyone as charming as Aunt Margaret having such a rude son. All he could do was stare and grunt. Obviously he couldn't carry on a conversation. Priscilla had done her best to draw him out in the car. She had followed all the rules for social conversation as laid out by Miss Barrett's social behavior class: "Discover a person's interests, then evidence an interest yourself, and he will begin talking." The fact that Edwin hadn't talked was probably due to the fact that he hadn't the brains to think of anything to say. She couldn't imagine anyone whose chief interest was rocks, anyway. Of course there had to be geologists in the world, and Priscilla could understand their absorption in the subject. But what would a grubby little boy know about geology?

She closed the suitcase and decided that politeness would not permit her to remain alone in her room any longer.

"Remember to be polite and considerate, dear," her mother had reminded her as she left the airport. "It's going to be very different from what you're used to. I've never been West myself, but your father used to tell me of it when he was a boy. His childhood was much different from mine."

"Of course I'll be polite and considerate, Mother," Priscilla had promised. But she hadn't known then about Edwin. Even Mother would find it hard to be polite to him.

Mrs. Herrick was shelling peas when Priscilla entered the kitchen, and the horrid boy was sitting at the table beside her, munching on cookies. His mouth was full of them, entirely too full, and before swallowing he crammed another one in. Priscilla pretended not to notice him.

"May I help you, Aunt Margaret?"

"I'm almost through, dear. Perhaps you'd like a cooky and a glass of milk?"

"No, thank you," said Priscilla quickly. "I had my lunch on the plane. I'm not used to eating between meals."

Edwin choked on a cooky, and again Priscilla looked away. He was so disgusting.

"This is such a pretty kitchen," she admired. "If I had a kitchen like this I'd want to spend a lot of time in it. Ours is tiny. It's only big enough for Mrs. Schmits, who cooks for us, but she doesn't like anyone in there bothering her, anyway."

"Thank you, Priscilla. We do spend a lot of time in here," said her aunt.

Priscilla sat down at the table and folded her hands in her lap. She felt suddenly awkward, as though she had run out of conversation. Everything was different, but not in the way she had expected it to be different. If her cousin weren't here, she might have mentioned the subject to Aunt Margaret, but of course she couldn't say anything now.

Her ideas of the West had been formulated on movies she had seen. There should be great rolling plains with rimrock cliffs, and herds of wild horses, and cowboys twirling ropes as they raced after stray steers. The towns should be small settlements of one-and two-story buildings, all lined up to face each other on a single street, with a tiny white church at one end. It had seemed picturesque and exciting, and she had considered herself lucky to be going to Oregon instead of California, for, as everyone knew, California was different, peopled as it was by the moving-picture industry and by eastern visitors who came to take the sun. Oregon was proving a great disappointment, for Portland was just another big city, and Aunt Margaret and the people she had glimpsed at the airport and on the streets would have fitted in inconspicuously at home. Only her cousin Edwin wouldn't fit in at home, and she doubted if he would fit in anywhere.

"Goodness, Ed," said his mother. "If you don't stop eating cookies, you're going to ruin your dinner."

"There's nothing else to do," he grunted. "You already said I couldn't go over to Duane's this afternoon."

"You'll have plenty of time to be with Duane later. I want you and Priscilla to get acquainted. Why don't you show her your rock collection?"

"She doesn't want to see it," said Edwin after a noticeable delay. Priscilla looked at him swiftly before looking away again. He must be a little smarter than she had given him credit for, or he wouldn't have sense enough to realize that.

"Nonsense," said Mrs. Herrick firmly. "Of course she does. Run along now, both of you."

Priscilla stood up obediently, and after a moment Edwin stood up too. She tried to look as though she were anticipating a pleasant experience, but it was hard to do.

"Come on," ordered Edwin gruffly.

She followed him down the basement stairs and paused when he did before a closed door.

"You don't have to pretend," he said frankly. "I know you don't know anything about geology. You can stall a minute, then go back upstairs. She won't know the difference. Anyway, my collection would be hard for you to understand."

Priscilla's chin came up angrily. There was a patronizing tone to his voice which she resented. She hadn't claimed to know anything about geology, but it was only from choice. Edwin was implying that she wasn't smart enough to grasp fundamentals.

"I'd love to see your collection," she insisted. "Aunt Margaret wants me to."

After a moment he opened the door and switched on the light. He didn't have manners enough to let her precede him, so she trailed along behind as he went in.

It was a small room with unfinished shelves

"I'd love to see your collection," she insisted. "Aunt Margaret wants me to."

across one side, on which were displayed neatly labeled specimens in various shapes, sizes, and colors. There was a center table overflowing with a collection of what appeared to be totally unrelated items—a half-empty vinegar bottle, a piece of broken window glass, a hammer and a chisel, a stack of newspapers, an unopened bottle of soda pop, a copper penny, a small bottle with a homemade label displaying a skull and crossbones and the warning "Poison! Hands off!!," a ball-point pen, a roll of adhesive tape, a fragment of bathroom tile, and a butcher knife. Under the high window stood a polishing wheel with a small motor which could be connected to a light socket.

"Well, now you've seen it," said Edwin, a little belligerently.

"Yes, I see," said Priscilla, struggling to keep her temper. She walked deliberately over to the shelf and began inspecting the specimens on display, reading the cards aloud. " 'Milky Quartz, May 3, 1957, found in gravel brought for back driveway.' 'Feldspar, May 3, 1957, found in gravel for driveway.' 'Mica, May 3, 1957, gravel driveway.' " She looked over her shoulder and smiled. "Well, at least you don't have to go very far to gather your rocks. You can just take them out of your own driveway."

"That's all you know," he said loudly. "Those three were the start of my collection. That's what got me interested, and that's why I saved them. I have better specimens of all those now. And anybody who knows anything at all would know better than to call those three specimens rocks, the way you did."

"What do you call them? Stones? Pebbles?"

"They're minerals," he said in a tone that made her want to take the rocks or minerals, or whatever they were, and throw them at him. "A mineral is a substance all by itself. A rock is a mixture of minerals. Any idiot ought to know that."

"How interesting," she said lightly, hoping he would realize that she didn't consider it interesting at all. She moved on down the shelf, pretending that his remarks hadn't stung a little. Suddenly she stopped. "There's some amethyst," she said in amazement. "I suppose you bought that."

"No, I found it," he told her proudly. "Last summer. Up at camp. There's a little there, but not too much."

"Oh." She put down the amethyst as though it were of no importance and picked up the thunderegg next to it. "What's this?"

"It's a thunderegg. You see, it looks like this on the outside." He showed her what appeared to be a shell of brownish-gray rock about the size of his fist. "You saw it open, like you would a geode, and it's filled with quartz-agate. When you polish it, you can see the picture."

She took the specimen in her hand and held it to the light. On a pearly white background, black lines traced a perfect replica of the surf rolling in on a sandy beach. There was even a small figure on the horizon which might be a ship far out at sea. The whole thing was as clearly etched as a photograph.

"How pretty," she said in real amazement.

"I found this too," he said, beaming proudly and taking another specimen from the shelf. "It's a geode with oil in it. We put it out in the hot sun, and real oil came out of it. But so far as they can prove, there's no oil up there in the Clarno Basin at all now."

This was not so interesting. It was just a piece of ugly gray rock which someone had taken the trouble to polish. Across the center of it ran a black smear. It formed no picture at all, and despite the polishing the rock wasn't really attractive.

"Oh," she said, making no motion to take it from him. Edwin scowled as he put it back on the shelf.

"Well, come on," he said with a return of his former gruffness, which made her realize that for at least two minutes he had been quite pleasant. "You've seen enough. Let's go back upstairs."

Mrs. Herrick was at the telephone when they returned to the kitchen, and it was evident that she was upset about something.

"I'll come as soon as I can," she was saying. "I don't think I can possibly leave tonight. There are certain arrangements which have to be made, but I can certainly leave by tomorrow. I'll fly, of course. Thank you for letting me know."

Her face, when she put down the receiver and turned to them, was very white.

"What's up, Mom?" asked Edwin anxiously.

"It's your grandmother. She's very ill. They've taken her to the hospital. I'll have to go to Pasadena tomorrow."

"Why can't you go tonight? You can phone Dad, or I'll tell him when he gets home from work. We'll be okay. I'll be going to camp Saturday anyway."

"I can't just leave," said Mrs. Herrick helplessly, and her eyes involuntarily turned to Priscilla. "I'll have to arrange for someone to come in and stay."

"What for?" demanded Edwin in a surprised tone. "Dad will be home nights, and *she*"—glancing at his cousin—"can cook for the two of them while you and I are gone."

"But I've never cooked in my life," gasped Priscilla before she thought. Mrs. Herrick didn't seem to hear, but Edwin looked at his cousin with undisguised scorn. She realized suddenly that she was the stumbling block which was keeping her aunt from leaving right now. Priscilla was a guest, a very new guest, and it wasn't polite to ask one's guest to take over the running of a house.

"But I can learn to cook, Aunt Margaret," she said swiftly. "You must have recipe books, and if Uncle Jim doesn't mind my experiments . . ."

"No, no, I wouldn't think of it," said Mrs. Herrick. "Jim can manage breakfast and take his dinners out. Eddie will be at camp. I wonder"—she seemed to be thinking aloud—"I wonder how you would like Camp Hancock."

"Mom!" gasped Edwin.

"Why, I think it would be very nice," said Priscilla brightly, trying to sound as though it were the very thing she wanted most of all. "I didn't realize there were girls at that camp too. I thought it was just for boys—boys like Edwin."

Three

For a full minute Ed could hardly believe that his mother was serious. The idea that this girl, his cousin, should even be considered in the same breath as the camp was preposterous. Camp Hancock was for serious people, for the dedicated scientists of tomorrow. It was no play camp, the entire purpose of which was to provide its campers with a good time. It was for workers. Even the girls at Camp Hancock—and there were a few, although boys predominated—were a little above the common garden-variety girls. They giggled less and usually attended to their own business. At times you could almost forget they were girls.

"It's full up, Mom," he said hastily, fearful of letting the idea grow in her mind. "They always have a waiting list. Maybe you could send her to a Camp Fire camp, or the Girl Scouts, or something like that. She wouldn't like this, and anyway, she wouldn't be eligible."

"I'm afraid that's so, Aunt Margaret," said Priscilla in that nicey-nice voice that Ed particularly hated. "I don't know the least thing about rocks."

"But you were telling me at the airport how interested you were in botany," remembered Mrs. Herrick. "Camp Hancock takes in several of the sciences. Unless, of course, you really don't want to go. Then we'd just have to think of something else."

"Oh, it isn't that," said Priscilla. Behind her aunt's back she gave Ed a look that made him want to sock her. "I think Edwin's camp sounds very interesting."

"Well, it won't hurt to try," decided Mrs. Herrick. "I'll call Mr. Hancock right now and explain the situation to him. Perhaps he can suggest something."

Ed couldn't stand it any longer. Without even excusing himself he turned and went outside. He wanted to yell or hit someone, preferably his cousin Priscilla. Since he knew he couldn't do that, he had to get away from her.

He sat down in the canvas lawn swing, pushing it back and forth with the tip of his tennis shoe, trying to decide what he should do. Obviously Mother couldn't, or wouldn't, realize that Priscilla was probably the worst thing that had ever happened to them. It was bad enough that she would be underfoot all summer when he returned from camp and that he'd have to put up with her around the house. He was reconciled to that, for he was sure that he could avoid her except at meals. But if she intruded on his two weeks at camp, he just didn't see how he could stand it. Field trips were open to anyone. He could just see her waiting until she found out where he was going, then signing up for the same trip. She'd probably tell everyone she was his cousin, and expect him to look after her, and maybe try to sit next to him around the campfire at night, or tag after him when they went to the swimming hole. And all the time she'd be chattering away in that affected voice of hers, making dumb remarks about Indians.

His thoughts were suddenly interrupted by a boy his own age, who appeared around the side of the house. It was his best friend, Duane Carpenter.

"Hi," said Duane in a low voice. "Didn't she come?"

"She came," admitted Ed sourly. "She's in the house, talking to Mom."

Duane opened the gate in the picket fence which encircled the back yard, and came over to join Ed in the lawn swing.

"How is she?" he asked.

"Bad. You can't imagine anything so bad. She's stuck up. And she's dumb, too."

"Well," said Duane philosophically, "some girls are, I guess."

"All girls are," said Ed quickly.

Duane was a good guy, his best friend, but he had to be kept firmly in line. He had a weakness

"Hi. Didn't she come?"

and, left to himself, he might give way to it. In a rash moment Duane had confessed that he thought a certain girl in their class was very pretty. Moreover, at dancing class, which they were both required to attend, Duane did not seem to hang back when it came time to select a new partner. Although Duane always denied it, Ed suspected that he actually enjoyed these contacts with members of the opposite sex.

"What does she look like?" asked Duane. "Is she good-looking?"

"No," scoffed Ed. "She's skinny. And she wears gloves and a hat. And she thought there'd be Indians walking around on the streets."

Duane laughed heartily, and Ed felt better. No Indians on the streets of a large city.

"The worst of it is," he confessed, "she might go to camp with us."

"Camp? You mean Camp Hancock? How can she?"

"Oh, she probably can't," said Ed. "It's just an idea of Mom's. She's telephoning Mr. Hancock about it now. But they've been filled up for a long time."

"Sure they have," said Duane. "They've been filled up for months. Why does she want to go to Camp Hancock?"

"She's got to go someplace. My grandma's sick. Mom has to go to Pasadena, and she can't just go off and leave Priscilla. She's too dumb to take care of herself, even if Dad would be here nights. I can see Mom's point. The only thing to do is to put Priscilla in some camp until she gets back. Only not Camp Hancock."

"Course not," agreed Duane loyally. Then in a whisper, "Hey, is that her?"

Ed glanced up and nodded briefly. Priscilla was standing in the kitchen doorway looking at them. She seemed to hesitate a moment, then she came outside and started down the steps toward them.

She had changed her clothes since her arrival, but she still looked too dressed up to suit Ed. Her cheeks were the same shade as her pink ruffled dress, and her straw-colored hair looked very bright in the sun as she tossed her head to make the pony tail switch around. She came straight toward them and stopped in front of the swing.

"I'm in the way in there," she said. "I think Aunt Margaret could talk more easily if I were out of the room."

"Oh," said Ed. After a moment he added a little grudgingly, "This is Duane Carpenter. This is Priscilla."

"Hi," said Duane. He shoved Ed, who was sitting in the middle of the swing, over in order to make room. "Why don't you sit down, Priscilla?"

"Thank you," said Priscilla in the approved dancing-school manner. She sat down beside Duane. "It's nice out here, isn't it?"

"Yeah," agreed Duane quickly. "It's nice. You came all the way on the plane, didn't you? Did you like it?"

"I like to fly," she agreed. "Of course you don't

get to see very much. I should think a train trip across the country would be more fun."

"I've been to San Francisco on the train," said Duane. "You do get to see a lot, especially if you're next to a window."

"I'd like that," said Priscilla. "I've never been on a train like that. We always have to fly because we always seem to be in a hurry. There's really not much to it."

Ed made a noise in his throat which was intended to show Duane that Priscilla was bragging, but Duane apparently didn't hear him. He went right on talking.

"Have you ever been out here before?"

"When I was a baby, but I was too little to remember. My father originally came from the West. He and Edwin's father were brothers, you know. But he died when I was only three, and Mother was always too busy to bring me. She's a buyer for a store. She's on a buying trip now in Paris."

"It's too bad you couldn't have gone with her," said Ed loudly.

"I wish I had now," said Priscilla in such a small voice that Ed could barely hear it.

"You'll have fun here," said Duane, "once you get used to it. You'll like it here. There are lots of things to do."

"What?"

"Well, we go swimming," began Duane thoughtfully.

"Oh, I love to swim," interrupted Priscilla. "Is the pool near here?"

"Not too near. We go on our bikes. It's too far to walk."

"She can walk to the wading pool," said Ed. "We used to go there when we were little kids, Priscilla. It'll be just right for you. Where we go it's pretty deep. You might drown."

"What else do you do in the summer?" asked Priscilla, ignoring Ed.

"Oh, we play ball, and sometimes tennis, and go to the beach or on hikes, and go to camp."

"Don't you ride?"

"Ride? You mean horses? They have horses for hire at the beach, and sometimes we ride there. But it's a buck an hour. You can't afford very much of that."

"I suppose you thought everybody had his own horse out here," suggested Ed. "And that you'd learn to be a good horseback rider before the summer was over."

Priscilla stood up, and her cheeks were even pinker than before.

"I am a good rider," she said quietly. She looked at Ed as though she intended to say something else, but evidently thought better of it. Then she smiled briefly at Duane. "Excuse me," she said, and turned and went into the house.

They stared after her, and when the screen door had closed Ed began to laugh.

"Did you hear that?" he demanded. " 'I am a good rider.' Did you ever hear such bragging in your life? What does she think we are, anyway? Where would she ever learn to ride?"

"I suppose there are riding schools back East," said Duane thoughtfully. "They have them here, only we just never went to one."

"Sure. Sure," laughed Ed. "Well, now you've seen her, you know why she couldn't go to Camp Hancock, don't you? All those fancy manners and all."

"Aw, come on," protested Duane. "She's not so bad. You aren't giving her a chance."

Ed glanced at him quickly. There was that weakness showing again.

"Let's go down to the rock room," he suggested. "I got to get my pack made up to take to camp."

It was possible to reach the basement without going through the main part of the house, and since the boys spent the remainder of the afternoon there, Ed did not see Priscilla or his mother until dinnertime. Duane decided it was time for him to go home when they heard Mr. Herrick's car drive into the garage, and shortly afterward Ed went upstairs.

They were all in the kitchen. Mrs. Herrick was taking something out of the oven. Mr. Herrick was leaning against the refrigerator, talking to her and Priscilla, who was bustling back and forth, carrying things into the dining room. Making herself right at home, Ed thought resentfully.

"Hi, Dad," he said, spearing an olive from the dish on the drainboard.

"Hello, Ed," said his father, raising his eyebrows slightly. "Where have you been? Your mother told you to stay home this afternoon and entertain your cousin."

"I was home," said Ed defensively. "I was in the basement with Duane. She could have come down there if she'd wanted to. I showed her the way once."

"Oh," said Mr. Herrick. He looked at Mrs. Herrick. "He was home, Margaret. You were mistaken about his running off somewhere."

"I'm sorry, Eddie," said his mother, giving him a quick hug as she went by. "I looked in the back yard as soon as I found out, and you were gone. I didn't even think to call."

"Found out what?" demanded Ed quickly. "What did you find out, Mom?"

"Why, your mother persuaded Mr. Hancock to make a place for Priscilla," said his father, smiling. "There was a cancellation, fortunately a girl camper, and when Mr. Hancock understood the circumstances he agreed that your cousin should have the place."

Priscilla snatched the dish of olives away just as Ed was on the point of reaching for it. Then she turned and held it out to him.

"I'm sorry," she said in a tone which let him understand that she wasn't at all. Moreover, he suspected that it wasn't olives she was talking about.

Four

Aunt Margaret took the afternoon plane to Pasadena the next day.

"Be good children," she said, kissing them both good-by. "Dad will be home at five-thirty to take you out to dinner. Be sure you're cleaned up, Eddie. I'm so sorry to have to rush away this way, Priscilla, but I'm sure you'll have a good time at camp. Eddie thought it was wonderful last year."

"It's all right, Aunt Margaret, and I'm sure I'll enjoy the camp," Priscilla assured her, but just the same she had a few misgivings as she watched her aunt go down the walk and get into the taxi which was to take her to the airport.

Out of the corner of her eye she could see her cousin waving wildly. He looked particularly disreputable this afternoon. He was wearing the same tee shirt he had worn yesterday, and while it had been clean when she first saw it, it had been steadily collecting grime ever since. His dark blue jeans had light spots at both knees where the fabric had worn thin, and his face and hands were distinctly dirty.

"By, Mom. Say hello to Grandma," he bellowed in a voice which could be heard all over the neighborhood. "If you see any good rocks, bring me some."

Mrs. Herrick smiled and waved, then the taxi carried her away.

"Well," said Priscilla, forcing a smile. After all, she supposed it was up to her to be polite to this obnoxious boy. "Is there something we should be doing this afternoon, Eddie? I mean, to get ready for camp tomorrow?"

"Don't call me Eddie," he said fiercely.

"It's what your mother calls you," she reminded him in some surprise.

"I know it. But don't you try. Don't you dare."

"You needn't shout so," she said indignantly. "I can hear perfectly well. What do you want me to call you? Edwin?"

"My name's Ed," he said shortly. "If you have to call me anything."

"Of course I'll have to call you something." It was very hard to keep her temper. "You're my cousin, and I have to stay here this summer. Don't think I want to, but I have to get along with you.

I have to pretend, especially to your mother and father, that I don't see anything wrong with you. That you're perfectly all right. As a matter of fact, I think you're quite impossible."

"Impossible?" He was staring with his mouth open so that she could see both rows of teeth. At least he must remember to keep them brushed, she thought to herself, or they couldn't be so white.

"Quite impossible," she said icily. "You're rude, and you're dirty."

"I suppose you think you're possible?" he gasped. "You with your gloves and your fancy airs! Maybe they're all right for a girl, but I don't like girls. I won't put up with them. Now that you've horned into my camp, you'd just better plan to stay out of my way when we get there. Don't be hanging around, expecting me to help you and telling everybody you're my cousin."

"You don't need to worry. I don't want anybody to know you're related to me, either." She forgot that young ladies did not raise their voices. She was yelling as loudly as he. "Why you'd think for a minute I'd want any help from you, I really can't imagine."

"Oh, you will," he shrieked. "You'll want help from anybody. What a helpless girl like you is going to do at Camp Hancock, I don't know. Or care, either." He turned to go into the house, then paused to shout over his shoulder, "When Duane comes, send him down to the basement."

Priscilla sat down in one of the porch chairs and was surprised to find that she was shaking with anger. What a horrible, dreadful, impossible boy. The idea of accusing her of horning into his camp! Did he think for a minute that she really wanted to go? After all, she was only being polite. It was Aunt Margaret's idea, not hers. And what was he talking about, insinuating that she would be unable to take care of herself? It was not the first time she had been to a camp. She had been to lots of them, and they were all very much alike.

She glared out at the tidy green lawn which yesterday had seemed so pleasant and now had become a mockery. It reminded her of the well-kept parks at home. She wished she were in one of them right now and that she could get up and walk to a familiar bus which would carry her to her own apartment house.

Someone was coming down the tree-lined street, and when he turned in at the walk she saw that it was Duane. He grinned at her in a friendly fashion, and she managed a weak smile in return. She wished Duane were her cousin instead of that horrible Ed.

"What's the matter?" asked Duane, stopping to inspect her critically. "You look sort of—funny."

"Nothing," she said airily. Her hands were still shaking a little, and her warm cheeks told her that her face was still flushed with anger. "I was just thinking, that's all. About that camp where we're going."

"Camp Hancock. It's swell," he assured her. "You'll like it."

"But what's it like?" she insisted. "Nobody's really told me much about it."

"It's pretty rustic," he admitted. "They don't have much money, you see. It hasn't been going very long, and everything is volunteered. It's up in eastern Oregon."

"Volunteered?" she repeated in amazement. "You mean it's a charity camp?"

"Oh no. We pay board, of course. But that just covers our food for two weeks and maintenance—you know, gasoline for the trucks, and stuff like that. It's sponsored by the Oregon Museum of Science and Industry, but nobody makes a profit."

"But I don't see—how about the counselors, the head of it, and the people who run it?"

"Volunteers, like I told you," he explained patiently. "The leaders are college professors mostly. They volunteer to take over a two-week session during the summer. I don't know who we'll get this year, but they're always good, so you don't need to worry. And there are a doctor and a nurse each session. They're volunteers, too. Mrs. Hancock does the cooking, and we kids do the work."

"I don't understand," she said helplessly, then drew herself up in dismay. Helpless was what Ed had accused her of being, and consequently helplessness must be avoided at all costs. Duane, however, didn't seem to notice.

"You will when you get there," he assured her. "You're lucky to get in. I don't think there's another camp like it in the United States. You see, it's for kids who are interested in science. Mr. Hancock started it a few years ago. He's a paleontologist, and——"

"Paleontologist?"

"Bones. Fossils," he explained. "I guess there's nothing about fossils that he doesn't know, and the Clarno Basin, where the camp is, is the greatest place to find them. You ought to see his collection."

"Are you studying to be a paleontologist?" she asked respectfully.

"No. Ed and I are rock hounds. You can study that, too, up there, and biology and astronomy and botany, or some of each. Ed says he guesses botany must be what sold Mr. Hancock on letting you come to camp. You must be pretty good."

Guiltily she tried to remember the conversation she had held with Aunt Margaret while they were waiting for Ed to fetch her bags at the airport. What in the world had she said? She remembered that Aunt Margaret had apologized for the fact that

Ed would be leaving for camp so soon after Priscilla arrived. It was a science camp, she had said; and Priscilla, feeling a little awkward and unsure before this new relative, had immediately gone on and on about the science course she had just completed in school. Botany had been interesting, and she had received a good grade, but she certainly didn't care to make a career of it.

"I have a lot to learn about it," she said, moistening her dry lips.

"Camp Hancock's the place to do that," he grinned.

"How do you get in? Who selects you?"

"It's usually done through the schools. You apply through the science classes. You're supposed to be between twelve and eighteen, but Ed and I made it last year when we were eleven."

"You must be very smart," she said absently. Suddenly she wished Duane would go away. Nice as he was, she needed to be alone, to have time to think things out. "Ed's in the basement. He said for you to come on down as soon as you got here."

She sat there after Duane had gone in the house, her thoughts racing around and around. Ed had been right, only he didn't know why he was right. She had no business attending a camp like Hancock, not because she was a girl, but because she wasn't a scientist. Moreover, she didn't want to be a scientist. Her interest in botany had ended with the grade on her report card, and when she tried now to recall some of the lessons, her mind was a perfect blank. Yet they would expect her to know something about the subject. At least they would expect her to be interested.

She got up and went down the steps into the front yard. Against the porch Aunt Margaret had planted a flower bed, all scarlet geraniums and white petunias. It was pretty and smelled good, but that was all it meant to her. She reached over and picked one of the blossoms, her mind searching for botanical terms. Stamen, pistil, where were they in this flower? And what were they? She couldn't remember, and after a moment she tossed the flower back into the bed with the others. She knew she was in trouble, and she didn't see at this point how she was going to avoid getting into more.

The rest of the day passed slowly. Ed and Duane spent the whole afternoon in the basement, and Priscilla sorted her clothes and packed what she needed for camp. Then she wrote a letter to her mother. She tried to make it gay, and she hoped it would sound as though she were having a good time. It was hard to do, and it took her a long time to complete, although the finished letter filled only a page of stationery.

Uncle Jim came home and took them out for dinner, and both Ed and Priscilla managed to hide their animosity. She found that it was easiest to do by not looking directly at her cousin and by addressing all her remarks to her uncle. Ed did the same thing, and Mr. Herrick had no idea that the two children had declared open warfare on each other only a few hours before.

"You'd better get to bed pretty early," he told them when they returned home. "That truck leaves at seven o'clock in the morning."

"Don't worry about me," said Ed loudly. "I'll be ready at six."

Priscilla began to think she'd never be able to sleep. She tossed and turned, worrying about what would happen tomorrow. How long would it take those experts to discover that her background in botany was inadequate? She could picture someone presenting her with a flower and demanding its Latin name and component parts. Then, when she couldn't give the correct answers, she would be accused of being there under false pretenses. How Ed would laugh, and how humiliated she would be.

At last an idea came to her, stemming from a chance remark of Duane's. He had said that campers might study any science they pleased. She would just have to stay far away from the botany sections and pretend an interest in something else. She could avoid her cousin in this way, too, since he would obviously devote himself to rocks. Having made up her mind on a course of action, she fell asleep, and the next thing she knew Uncle Jim was calling that there was just time to eat breakfast before they left for the truck.

It was the first time that Priscilla had ever ridden in a truck. There were two of them, one a light panel truck, like the kind used for deliveries of merchandise in the city, the other a little larger, of the type used by farmers to haul produce, with an open bed behind the driver's seat. Uncle Jim tossed her bedroll into the larger truck and grinned at her.

"You'd better sit in this one," he said. "The spring won't be good, but at least you'll have a chance to see the country."

A crowd had already collected by the time they arrived, and he had to raise his voice to make himself heard. Everyone seemed to be talking and laughing at once; and, worst of all, everyone but Priscilla seemed to be acquainted with everyone else. She looked around her, feeling a little panicky. At this moment she would have been thankful even for Ed, but he had disappeared somewhere in the crowd.

"You'd better take your seat so you can get a good spot," said Uncle Jim. "Pretty soon they'll all be getting on and you won't have a choice."

Since there were no seats at all on the truck bed, she realized she was supposed to make her own, using her bedroll. She climbed up, stepping over other people's bedrolls, until she came to her own, which she placed near the front. Uncle Jim came around and stood next to the truck, smiling up at her encouragingly.

"Okay," shouted a man's voice. "Let's go. All aboard."

Instantly there was a mad scramble as the two trucks began to fill with bedrolls and their owners. Mothers and fathers crowded closely alongside, calling last-minute instructions and good-bys. Priscilla sat quietly, hoping no one could hear how loudly her heart was thumping. She was thinking that it might have been better to find a place in the

Priscilla found herself staring into the sunburned face of a girl about her own age

other truck, despite the fact that the sides would have obstructed her view, for this one seemed to be filling up with boys. At that moment she felt herself being pushed over against the side as another bedroll was jammed down on the floor between hers and the one next to it. Then someone plopped down on top of the bedroll, and she found herself staring into the sunburned face of a girl about her own age. She had curly black hair, cut short, and twinkling gray eyes, and she wore, as did almost all the other campers, sturdy jeans and a cotton shirt.

"Hi," said the girl. "I saw you up here. I guess you and I are the only ones who can hold our own. The other girls had to ride in the panel."

"I was the first one on," explained Priscilla.

"That's smart," approved the girl, wriggling down, to make herself more comfortable. "I'm Ginny. Virginia Gregory. What's your name?"

"Priscilla Herrick."

"Not Eddie's sister?" asked Ginny curiously. "He doesn't have a sister, does he?"

"He's my cousin," explained Priscilla, wishing she didn't have to. "I'm spending the summer with his mother and father. I never laid eyes on him before Thursday."

"Eddie's okay," said Ginny tolerantly. "You just have to smack him down once in a while, that's all. You ever been to Camp Hancock before?"

"No."

"It's swell," began Ginny, but as the driver started his motor that instant, she forgot about Priscilla and turned to shriek good-bys to someone in the crowd.

Priscilla became increasingly grateful for

Ginny's company as they drove along. True, she yelled as loudly as any of the boys on the truck, and Miss Barrett might not approve of her, but Priscilla liked her. There was something genuine about Ginny Gregory. She would be a comforting friend to have and, most of all, Priscilla needed a friend right now.

More than once during the trip she was thankful that Uncle Jim had tossed her sleeping bag onto the open truck, otherwise she would never have been able to see the country. Everything was strange to her. First they passed through miles given over to small farms. Signs along the road proclaimed, "Berry Pickers Wanted," and in the fields she could see men, women, and children bending over rows of vines as they gathered the fruit. Then the farms gave way to the beginnings of the forest, and the highway curved up and in and out of the tallest, thickest fir trees Priscilla had ever seen.

"It's the Mount Hood National Forest," Ginny explained when she asked her. "Nobody's allowed to log here. That's why they're so thick. We'll pass right by Mount Hood, so you can get a good view of where we ski in the wintertime. I'll show you."

"Then this must be the Cascades," said Priscilla, remembering her geography. "I didn't realize that Camp Hancock was in the mountains."

"It isn't," said Ginny promptly. "We'll go

Priscilla became increasingly grateful for Ginny's company as they drove along

right down the other side. It's not like this at all. You'll see."

At Government Camp the truck paused for fifteen minutes, and everyone piled out to get a cool drink. Priscilla was relieved that Ginny obviously intended to stay with her. She grasped Priscilla's arm firmly and pushed her along through the crowd, all of whom were trying to find places at the counter at once. It was exciting, if a little breath-taking, and before she knew it Priscilla was elbowing her way forward as enthusiastically as Ginny.

"Hey, watch out!" said a familiar voice, and she realized with dismay that her last energetic push had landed in the back of her cousin Ed.

He turned, grinning good-naturedly, but his smile faded when he recognized her.

"Quit following me," he snapped. "I warned you about that. You'd better remember what I said, too."

"What's the matter, Eddie?" asked Ginny cheerfully. "Got a stomach-ache?"

"Yeah," grunted Ed, managing to move away in the crowd. "I get one every time I look at her."

"What's eating him?" demanded Ginny in surprise. "Is he mad at you or something?"

"He doesn't like me. And I don't like him, either. He's rude, and he always looks dirty, and he thinks he knows everything, and he doesn't."

"Oh, sure," agreed Ginny. "Lots of boys are like that. You've got to overlook it. Why doesn't he like you?"

"Because I had to come to Camp Hancock, and he thinks it belongs to him," explained Priscilla. "You see, Aunt Margaret had to go out of town, and there wasn't anyplace else for me to go. Ed's afraid I'll embarrass him, I guess. The worst of it is, I probably will."

"Don't be silly," said Ginny. "Let's get our drink. What do you want? Orange or cherry?"

Priscilla had never seen a snow-capped mountain near at hand. Mount Hood towered above the tree tops along the highway, so close that it seemed she ought to be able to reach out and touch it. She could see the glaciers, the huge rocks from which snow had blown or had melted under the July sun, and long stretches of glistening white, so thick and deep that they had never completely melted. Then Mount Hood was behind them, and once more they were in the cool, fir-scented forest, only this time they were going down, not up. The driver had to brake his truck to keep it from running away. The giant firs, interspersed on this slope with pine, crowded closely on either side of the highway, their tops almost meeting overhead, and then, without warning, the trees began to thin out, and sunshine poured down on the highway.

"We're getting there," announced Ginny in satisfaction.

"To Camp Hancock?"

"Oh no. That's still a couple of hours away. But we're in eastern Oregon now."

Priscilla caught her breath. They were even with the last of the forest, and ahead was spread another world, all brown and gold under a dazzling blue sky. Against the horizon was a flat-topped cliff, which looked as though someone had leveled it off with a knife, and below one side of the highway lay a canyon where grew only an occasional low scraggling tree or a cluster of grayish-green vegetation. It had been cool in the forest, but here the sun beat down piteously, trying to extract nonexistent moisture from an already dry land. It was exactly as she had seen it in the movies, the Far West of Wyatt Earp and Buffalo Bill. She felt that at any moment an Indian scout might appear silhouetted against the rimrock ledge, or that a herd of wild horses might stampede their way out of the canyon.

"Is Camp Hancock like this?" she asked Ginny with shining eyes. "I mean, is it in a place like this?"

"Sure," agreed Ginny. "All eastern Oregon's alike, except where there's water. You'll like it."

"I know I will," said Priscilla happily. For the first time since she had arrived she was really glad she had come.

Five

Ed scrambled over the side of the truck and jumped to the ground. Through the thin rubber soles of his tennis shoes his feet stung with the hard impact against the ground, but he hardly noticed.

It was good to be back. His eyes ran over the familiar landmarks, over the clusters of tents, those for the boys on the left, the girls' on the right, and those which were used as workrooms in the middle. They were the same tents as last year, a little more faded perhaps, with here and there a new patch, but exactly the same. There was the flagpole, topped by the Stars and Stripes, which was raised precisely at six-thirty each morning and lowered when the sun slid over the blue line of the Cascades to the west. There was only one permanent structure, a mess hall, built from the lumber of an old house which had been torn down in the nearby small town of Clarno. It was open at the sides, and he could see that the long tables stretching from one end to the other were already laid for lunch. There would be no sandwiches in a sack today. They would eat in camp before they started their hike.

He wondered where he and Duane should go on this first afternoon. There were so many places he wanted to revisit, so many treasures hidden in the surrounding cliffs and canyons. Perhaps they should go to the agate beds north of camp, or to the nut beds down by what was once, millions of years ago, an ancient swamp. There he might be lucky enough to find a petrified pecan or a black walnut or an acorn. Or, if there was time, they could go clear to Old Glory Rock and look for zeolites. The possibilities were endless, and it was hard to make a choice.

"Come on," said Duane, yanking on his arm. "There's Mr. Hancock. Let's go say hello and find our tent."

It was easier to say than to do. Everyone wanted to speak to the founder of Camp Hancock at once, particularly those who were returning for their second, third, or fourth time. He was a slight, wiry man of medium height, with white hair and pink cheeks, and had he been given the extra poundage and a white beard, he would have made a creditable Santa Claus at Christmas time. His blue eyes twinkled with all the tireless enthusiasm of the

There was no mistaking the heartiness of his welcome

youngest camper, and there was no mistaking the heartiness of his welcome.

"Roger! It's good to see you. Bill, you've grown six inches since last summer. Andy, I still owe you a dunking from last summer. Just wait till I get you down to the swimming hole!"

Duane was trying to inch his way forward into the reluctantly moving knot of boys surrounding Mr. Hancock, and he turned with surprise when he felt Ed pulling him back.

"What's the matter?"

"Let *them* get out first," said Ed, frowning.

Ginny Gregory and his cousin were next in line to meet Mr. Hancock, and Ginny was introducing Priscilla to him at that very moment.

Ed had been a little surprised to see how well the two seemed to get along on the truck. Of all the girls of his acquaintance, Ginny was the most tolerable. She didn't giggle, and he had a sneaking suspicion that she resented dancing school as much as he. She wasn't always fussing about her appearance, either, combing her hair and fooling with her dress. He couldn't imagine how Ginny Gregory could put up with anyone like Priscilla.

Suddenly it seemed to him that Mr. Hancock's voice boomed over the obbligato of chattering with unnecessary loudness.

"So you're Ed Herrick's cousin. Well, we're mighty glad to have you with us, Priscilla. Ed's one of our best young scientists. You're lucky to have him to get you started in the right direction."

Ed felt his ears grow warm, and he glared belligerently in every direction. To his surprise, no one seemed to notice. For the first time in his life he felt a little resentment toward Mr. Hancock. Usually there was no one more understanding or sympathetic. Did he actually think that Ed intended to spend his two weeks baby-sitting with a girl?

Priscilla answered in such a low voice that Ed couldn't hear what she said, but he caught Mr. Hancock's next remark.

"As a matter of fact, I was glad when Mrs. Herrick called. We'd just had a cancellation from a twelve-year-old girl. That left Ginny here the only girl that age in this session. The other girls are all older, and I thought she'd need a chum."

So that was it! That was why Priscilla had been accepted, as a partner for Ginny Gregory. Ed forgot that he had almost liked Ginny before. At the moment he almost hated her.

In a few minutes Priscilla and Ginny moved on. His resentment continued to smolder until it was his turn to shake Mr. Hancock's hand, then it was immediately forgotten in the warmth of those kind blue eyes.

"Guess what we've saved for this afternoon, boys," said Mr. Hancock. "The blasting!"

"The blasting!" repeated Ed in delight.

"We thought we'd miss it in the second session," said Duane. "You always start off with it."

"I know, and we did. Blasted off a big hunk the first day," agreed Mr. Hancock. "But you never saw such a bunch of eager beavers as there were in that first session. They went through those beds in nothing flat."

"Where'll it be?" demanded Ed. "And when?"

"The nut beds, of course," smiled Mr. Hancock. "Soon as we finish lunch. And that'll be just as soon as you've stowed away your gear and tidied up."

It didn't take long to settle themselves in their tent. Ed and Duane each selected one of the eight cots and unrolled their sleeping bags on top. The few toilet articles they had brought—toothbrushes, combs, and soap—went underneath, as did changes of underwear, towels, and clean shirts. Camp Hancock was rustic, but the boys knew from experience that they and their belongings had to be kept clean and neat.

Lunch was a hilarious affair, but today the leaders and counselors only grinned tolerantly. They knew that such pandemonium was caused by the excitement of the arrival. It wouldn't always be like this at mealtime. In the midst of it Ed looked down the other side of the table and caught a glimpse of his cousin. She was eating quietly, her face set in that polite little smile of hers. Ginny, beside her, was carrying on a conversation with someone across the table. Priscilla looked a little scared and uncomfortable, but it was her own fault. She shouldn't have come in the first place.

When everyone had finished, Mr. Hancock stood up.

"Most of you have heard that I'm planning a little blasting for this afternoon," he announced, smiling. "Anybody who cares to watch can come along, but if you're too tired from the long ride you're welcome to stay in camp and rest up. The only thing is, KP lists are posted there on the wall. Dishes have to be washed, you know, and cans flattened and garbage carried away and buried. We'll put off the start for half an hour, in case anyone who has a job to do wants to come along."

There was a surge for the bulletin board, and those who got there first began calling out the names of those who were scheduled to clear up after lunch.

"Not us," said Duane with satisfaction when the last name had been read. "We missed it this time, but they'll probably catch us at dinner."

"Then we might as well start out for the nut beds now," decided Ed. "It's a long walk. The others will catch up."

They started out in companionable silence, their tennis shoes making occasional little plopping sounds on the hard ground. It was a funny thing, Ed decided, about being up here. You thought nothing of hiking miles; you even chose to do so. Back home he insisted on riding his bicycle or being driven everywhere in a car, for even such a short jaunt as to the neighboring grocery store. He guessed it was because this was so much more interesting.

Over there in the north was old Iron Mountain, looking like a pointed cone of chocolate ice cream against the blue sky. What a humbug it was and how it managed to fool everyone, for what looked like a mountain from here was nothing but a level rimrock plateau rolling back to the Columbia. Moreover, there was neither iron nor minerals of any kind there, nothing but rattlesnakes and an occasional arrowhead from a long-deserted Indian camp. And there were the Red Hills, and behind him, towering above that incongruous green splotch which marked the swamp, were the Palisades, both of them rimrock, to be sure, but viewed from a distance through the dry heat waves of the afternoon, they seemed to be something of enchantment. He felt a little silly when he realized he was thinking of enchantment, as though he were still a little boy and not twelve years old.

"Sure is nice to be back," said Duane. "I plan to get a lot of specimens this summer. Really build up my collection."

"Me too. I hope I find a good geode."

"We probably should have started right away. We've only got two weeks."

"And miss the blasting?" cried Ed in horror.

They took their time, and as they reached the nut beds the others were beginning to catch up with them. At first glance there was little to distinguish these overhanging cliffs from any of the others. They were sedimentary rock; that is, rocks made from solid particles laid down by the action of water. They were variegated in color, with patches or stripes of gray, brown, tan, even red and black, but so skillfully were they blended that one had to look twice to see where one color left off and the next began. From where the campers were standing at the bottom, the cliff rose to heights of fifty and a hundred feet, and the ground underfoot was scattered with hunks and portions of the same rock. This was obviously not the first time blasting had taken place at this point.

"You know," said Ed, squinting professionally as he looked up. "That rock is sure stratified. It sure is."

"Of course it is," agreed Duane placidly. "Or it wouldn't be sedimentary rock, idiot. It has to be made in layers. There's no other way for water to make it."

"I mean, you can't always see it as plainly as you can from here," explained Ed with dignity. "We can get some good mineral specimens when it's all over, even if we don't find a nut—shale and sandstone and mica."

Mr. Hancock came hurrying up, shaking his head in mock dismay.

"You people have come too far," he accused. "You must have left camp before I had time to finish my instructions. I want you back, way back with those others. You can't stand right under a cliff when somebody's going to dynamite it. Mr. Martin's all ready to set off the charge, and he can't do a thing until you get back out of the way. After things have settled down, you can come back and pick up enough nuts to fill your baskets."

They laughed appreciatively at the joke. Being experienced campers, they knew they would have to pick the nuts out of the hard pieces of rock with their hammers, if they were lucky enough to find any at all.

When he was sure that they were safely away, Mr. Martin bent over and applied a match to the fuse. Then he, too, dashed back as fast as he could.

"There she goes. She's going—going—" said a voice next to Ed, and automatically he glanced over and saw that he was standing beside Ginny Gregory. In that one second he saw that her eyes were glistening with excitement and that on the other side of her was the startled face of Priscilla. He had no further time to think of them. He looked back.

There was a spurt of flame, a great crashing roar which shook the ground, and the side of the cliff seemed to explode. In a cloud of dust and flying particles, a great portion of the side cracked off and went tumbling, crashing to the ground.

"Oh!" exhaled the watching campers in such a timed exclamation that they might have been following the baton of an orchestra leader.

"Hold it!" warned Mr. Hancock. "Give it time to settle and to see if any more is going to crack off. Don't rush up there too soon."

It was then that Ed glanced again at his cousin. To his surprise, she hadn't covered her face with her hands as he had seen some girls do upon witnessing their first dynamite charge. She was just staring, sort of bug-eyed, as though she wondered what was going to happen next.

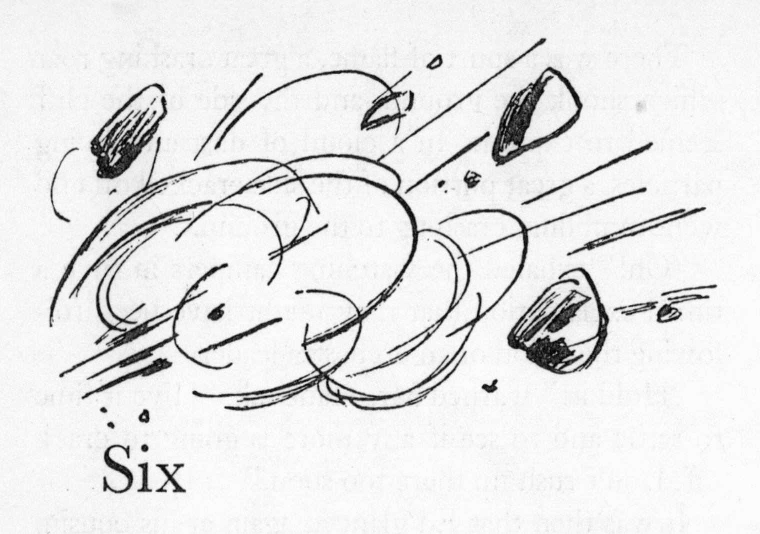

Six

Priscilla had never witnessed an actual dynamiting before. Of course she had seen it in the movies and on television, so she had an idea of what to expect, but it still seemed unreal. At first she had thought they were standing too far back to get a good view, but as the sound of the explosion filled the air and she saw jagged fragments of rock propelled upward against the blue sky, she was afraid they were too close. Her instinct told her to run, but her feet were frozen to the trembling ground.

She couldn't see the effects of the charge immediately, for the cloud of dust hovered thickly about the cliff for some time. Little by little it began to dissolve, then she realized the smell of powder and dust had filled her nose and she was grinding dust between her teeth. It was spreading out in every direction.

For the second time Mr. Hancock called that they were to stay where they were until he had made sure it was safe for them to go up to the cliff.

"We could sit down," said Ginny sensibly. "He's awfully particular. It will take him a while to make sure there aren't any loose places on the cliff that might come down on our heads. How did you like it?"

"It was—interesting," said Priscilla cautiously. "But I didn't know they were planning to dynamite a cliff. I thought we were going to the nut beds."

"That is the nut beds," agreed Ginny. "That whole cliff that they dynamited."

"But I thought nuts grew on trees, or at least bushes. And there isn't one in sight."

"We have to dig them out," explained Ginny. "There used to be trees there. Sometimes we find pieces of the wood, petrified, of course. Oak and black walnut, and trees without any rings in the wood, so you can tell they grew in a time when there weren't any seasons. The nuts are fossils."

Ed would have laughed at her for being so stupid, and Priscilla was grateful to Ginny for taking her ignorance in such a matter-of-fact way, but she still felt called upon to apologize.

"I'm afraid I'm awfully stupid. I didn't realize we were looking for fossils. I thought that we were looking for rocks. Not that it would make much difference," she admitted ruefully. "I don't know much about either one of them."

"You will by the time you leave," Ginny assured her. "Everybody does. This is the only way to learn about these things, really. Even those who've spent all winter reading books don't know everything when they get here. They may think they do, but they find out differently. And even then they can make a mistake."

"I wish I did know a little something about rocks," said Priscilla wistfully. "But of course there are so many. I don't see how you ever keep them straight."

"There are just two kinds of rocks, really. Igneous and sedimentary," Ginny explained. Then, warming to her subject, "You see, all rocks come from inside the earth. It's called magma there, and rocks made by fire—by liquid lava and magma—are igneous rocks. They were the first rocks on earth. After a while heat and cold, rain and snow began to wear away the igneous rocks, and the little particles of sand and mud were carried away by rivers and oceans. The weight of the sand above squeezed them together, and the chemicals in the water sort of cemented them, and they made a new rock. That's called sedimentary. That's what these cliffs are made of."

"But there aren't any rivers or oceans here."

"Not now, but there were. This was all covered by an ocean once. We've found fossils of sea dinosaurs around here, and shells and things like that. Then the ocean dried up or went away, and there was a swamp. There were trees then, and there must have been a forest standing on this very spot, because we've found so many nut fossils here."

"Do you mean you can find fossils in any of these cliffs?" gasped Priscilla. "All you have to do is dig them out?"

"Oh, you won't find them in every one. You could dig some of them flat to the ground and you wouldn't find a fossil or anything. And then in another cliff, maybe a half mile away, you'd find a whole bed of them. The mammal beds are places where the first mammals used to congregate for some reason or other, maybe to eat or sun themselves. We've found two mammal beds, but we haven't found a real dinosaur bed yet."

"Do you think you will?"

"Of course," agreed Ginny cheerfully. "We just haven't looked in the right places, that's all. They found a bone of a brontothere around here. That's the thunderbeast. It came right after the true dinosaur. And we found a leg bone of the three-toed horse. All we've got to do is keep on looking. We'll find a real dinosaur."

"Goodness," said Priscilla. "Do you suppose we'll find a nut fossil today?"

"We might," agreed Ginny. "I wouldn't turn up my nose at one. But what I really want to find this trip is a good geode."

"What's that?"

"It's a rock with a crystal inside. It's hard to find."

Mr. Hancock signaled from the cliff that it was now safe for the campers, and everyone rushed forward, Priscilla with them. She wasn't exactly sure what she was looking for, and she was afraid she wouldn't recognize a fossil nut if she saw one, but she was determined to do her best.

The ground beneath the cliff was now littered with rocks. There were large boulders and small ones, and in some places the dynamite charge had reduced the once solid cliff into fragments the size of pebbles.

"I should think this would just blow up the whole fossil," puzzled Priscilla, imitating Ginny, who had selected the pebble-sized pile and was now poking diligently about in it.

"Oh, he wouldn't dynamite the mammal beds," said Ginny quickly. "Mammals are too big. But nuts are so tiny, you aren't so likely to hurt them. Besides, lots of them have already been found. Mammals and dinosaurs aren't so common."

Priscilla began to search fervently. If only she

Mr. Hancock signaled from the cliff that it was now safe for the campers

could find a nut, a rare one that no one had discovered before. Even that horrible Ed would be impressed then. Suddenly her eye was caught by something sparkling like a mirror in the pile of grayish-brown rocks. She picked it up quickly.

It wasn't a nut, but it had to be something valuable

The shining something seemed to be a streak in another rock, and obviously it had been split off from a larger piece. It wasn't a nut, but it had to be something valuable.

"Ginny!"

Ginny looked up.

"Find something?" she asked.

Priscilla held it out to her silently. Ginny inspected it carefully, digging at it a little with her fingernail.

"It's a good specimen of mica," she agreed. "See

how it splits off in layers? You ought to use it to start your collection."

"What's mica?" asked Priscilla in disappointment. It couldn't be too rare or Ginny would have been more excited.

"It's a mineral. The little window you see in light fuses is mica. That's where I got my first specimen. In Russia, a long time ago, they used mica for windowpanes and called it muscovite. That's a good specimen you found. I've never found as big a piece myself."

"It's pretty common, I suppose?"

"Oh yes. But don't throw it away. You aren't likely to find another piece that big around here, and you can't have a collection without one."

Priscilla slipped it into her pocket a little resentfully. Of course she intended to keep it, at least for a little while. Even if it was common, it was pretty. But she had no intention of making a collection. Ed would think she was copying him.

They poked around in the boulders for another hour and a half, until the heat of midafternoon finally drove them back to camp. No one had unearthed a petrified nut, but to Priscilla's surprise no one seemed discouraged.

"It takes a long time," Ginny explained. "You have to keep going over and over the same ground, because maybe it's been staring you right in the face all the time and you didn't see it."

"Will we look there again tomorrow?"

"Some of them will. But tomorrow we'll break up in small groups and start looking for the things in which we're most interested. I'm going to start looking for a geode. Do you want to come along."

"I'd like to," said Priscilla quickly. She felt safer in Ginny's company than she would have if she had to go out on her own.

Seven

When his curved fingers touched the stake, Ed obediently turned over in the water and started floating back. The stake was as far as the campers were allowed to swim in this direction, and the edge of the bridge marked the opposite boundary line. It was a fine swimming hole, for at this point the John Day River formed a slow whirlpool over a deep basin which usually provided plenty of room for everybody.

It was a very satisfactory first day, he thought contentedly, enjoying the pleasant lap of the water against his cheek. First the arrival to find everything just as he had left it, then the dynamiting, now the midafternoon swim. He had never seen so many pile onto the trucks as when they left for the river. Usually a few remained behind in camp, but today every man, woman, and child had appeared in a bathing suit, with a towel over his arm. The camp was completely deserted, and the swimming hole was well filled. Too well filled, he thought as his head came up against an unyielding object, and he went completely under.

He came up immediately and saw that he had bumped heads with another floater.

"You ought to watch where you're going," he said mildly.

"I wasn't born with eyes in the top of my head like a frog," said Ginny Gregory, treading water and rubbing the spot he had bumped. "Hey, have you seen your cousin dive? I bet she could make the Olympic team if she tried out!"

"I haven't noticed," said Ed, scowling. He thrashed away, splashing an unnecessary amount of spray just because it made him feel better.

He had seen Priscilla dive all right, and swim, too; and much as he hated to admit it, she was pretty fair for a girl. She had been showing off ever since they came, racing with some of the best swimmers in camp, and beating them, too. But it was probably just a freak day. No girl could compete with boys and expect to win all the time.

He glared, remembering a moment earlier in the afternoon when he and Priscilla had happened to meet at the stake at the boundary line.

"I hope you think it will be safe for me to go

in the wading pool alone, Ed," she had told him sweetly.

He had splashed furiously away, remembering what he had said to her that day in the lawn swing. Well, how could he have known she was a fair swimmer? She hadn't looked much like one then.

Duane was sitting on the bank with another boy, and Ed made his way toward them as fast as he could.

"Hey, you guys aren't getting out already?" he accused, standing over them and bombarding them with little drops as he shook himself.

"Sure thing," answered the other boy. He was one of the older campers, perhaps sixteen or seventeen. Ed didn't know much about him outside of the fact that his name was Tom and that he had been here last year. "Mr. Hancock says we'll have to go back to camp pretty soon now."

"All the more reason to swim while you can," pointed out Ed quickly. "You won't have a chance again until tomorrow."

"Maybe you forgot, kid, or maybe this is your first trip," said Tom good-naturedly, "but if you get in the truck damp, the dust from the road will turn into mud all over you."

Usually Ed didn't try to argue with the older boys, but this one didn't make sense.

"What difference does that make?" he asked in a puzzled voice.

Tom just grinned and shrugged, without bothering to answer. Ed sat down beside Duane.

"Aren't you going back in, either? Or are you afraid of a little mud?"

"In a minute," agreed Duane hastily. "Priscilla's going to do a swan dive. I want to watch that first."

"Priscilla? Swan dive?"

"She's good," said Duane enthusiastically. "Haven't you seen her?"

"No," said Ed shortly.

"She's darn good," approved Tom. "Cute little kid, too. She's got on a white bathing suit and a cap with flowers on it. Maybe you noticed her even if you didn't see her dive."

"Oh, I know who she is," admitted Ed reluctantly.

"He ought to. She's his cousin," said Duane, and looked surprised when Ed glared at him.

"Is that so?" Tom raised his eyebrows. Then he turned and looked over his shoulder. "Where'd she go, anyway? She isn't back at the board. And she said she'd show us the swan."

"Maybe she was just talking. Girls do that, you know," Ed reminded them. "Probably she can't do a swan at all. She——"

"There she is," cried Duane, jumping to his feet. "She's down by the bridge. Hey, she can't dive from there. It's out of bounds!" He lifted his voice and began calling at the top of his lungs. "Priscilla! Priscilla! Come back! Don't dive there!"

Priscilla was too far away to hear, but nearly everyone else did. Duane's voice carried over the water. It rose above the sounds of splashing and the chatter of those who were drying off on the bank. People glanced first at Duane, then toward the bridge which crossed the John Day.

A girl in a white bathing suit and cap was standing on the railing high above the river. She looked

"Hey, she can't dive from there. It's out of bounds."

small against the immense backdrop of blue sky. On this side, the water was smooth and green, but as it broke under the bridge it was dotted with flecks of white which bespoke jagged rocks that caught and tore the current.

"She's diving on this side," muttered Tom. "She'll come down in the hole, but just the same it's dangerous. Somebody ought to stop her."

Yes, somebody should stop her, and Ed realized that the somebody was he. Much as he resented it, she was his cousin. To a certain extent she was his responsibility—at least his mother and father considered her so. How would he ever explain things to them if she broke her back or killed herself in such a dive? He tried to call out, but his voice came back in a tiny squeak.

At that moment Priscilla made the dive. They saw her spring out, and then her body curved and bent. Down, down she went, straightening at just the right moment to cut the deep, smooth surface at the outer boundary of the pool.

The campers cheered. They whistled and clapped and screamed. All but Ed. A moment before he had been cold with fear; now he was burning with rage. The show-off! Who did she think she was, anyway? What was she trying to prove? That she was better than anyone else?

Priscilla was swimming upstream now, her arms cutting the water with strong, swift strokes. She's coming right up here, Ed thought angrily. She's coming right up on this spot on the bank where I am, expecting me to tell her how good she is. Then he realized that he was not the reason why Priscilla was heading in his direction. Mr. Hancock was standing on the bank just a little above the spot where the three boys had been sitting, and Mr. Hancock was waving Priscilla in.

A few moments later she came up on the bank, breathless and flushed with excitement, trailing little streams of water behind her.

"That was a beautiful dive, Priscilla," said Mr. Hancock gently. "But I don't want you to do it again."

"But I made the dive inside the limits," she protested. "You said we could go as far down as the bridge. I didn't go any farther."

"We never made a rule about anyone diving off the bridge because we didn't think it would occur to anyone," he explained. "It's a little too high to be safe, and if someone who wasn't as experienced as you tried it, he might be in pretty bad trouble. From now on, diving from the bridge is out of bounds for everyone."

"I'm sorry, Mr. Hancock," said Priscilla. She was using that nicey-nice voice of hers, Ed thought disapprovingly, trying to make people think she was all strawberries and cream. "I didn't think of that. Of course I won't do it again."

"It was a swell dive, though," said Tom enthusiastically.

"Show-off," muttered Ed in a voice which was quite audible to everyone. He turned and stalked away as fast as he could.

To be perfectly honest, he had never seen a better dive. He knew he couldn't have done as well himself, but he still thought Priscilla was a show-off. He dived back into the pool and swam energetically back and forth until it was time to return to camp. At least his cousin had the decency to stay out of the water for the rest of the day. He saw her sitting quietly on the bank by herself.

It was two miles over a rough dirt road from the swimming hole to the camp, and Tom had been right about the road dust turning to mud on damp skin. Even those who had taken care to dry themselves thoroughly before climbing into the truck were coated with a film of dust by the time they reached their destination. Ed, who hadn't bothered to dry off at all, was black from the crown of his head to his bare feet.

"Looks as if you'll have to do a complete scrub-up job before dinner," Mr. Graves, the new leader of the geology group, told him as he jumped off the truck. "Maybe you ought to start now, so you'll be through in time."

"Oh, I'll make it, sir," laughed Ed tolerantly. Since Mr. Graves was so new, he didn't realize that lots of campers returned from swimming dirtier than when they had left. Just the same, he might as well get cleaned up now. It would have to be done eventually, and he might miss something later on if he stalled.

He went to his tent after soap and a dry towel, and the moment he stepped inside he was struck with the feeling that something was wrong. Things weren't exactly as he had left them, and for a full minute he didn't realize what accounted for the change. Then he realized that his cot was bare. The sleeping bag, which he had unrolled and spread out on top, was no longer there.

Someone must be playing a joke on him. Someone had hidden his sleeping bag and even now might be lurking around outside waiting for him to make an uproar. It must be one of the new campers, for no one who had been there before would do such a thing. For the moment he decided to do nothing about it at all. Before long, whoever had done it would realize it wasn't such a funny joke after all and would return the bag, probably without saying anything.

He carried his soap and towel outside to tackle the washing up. Mr. Graves was right. It was something of a job, for he had to use cold water in a tin basin. There was a single shower in camp, but he would have to wait in line, and it wasn't worth it. When he had finished, he replaced the soap and towel in his tent, giving a quick glance at his cot. The sleeping bag was still missing. Well, give them time. It would come back pretty soon.

A crowd was collecting around the unlighted campfire, already laid in readiness for the evening. Off at one side a couple of boys were tossing horseshoes, and there were both checkers and monopoly games going. Tonight there was none of the boisterousness which had characterized the day's lunch. The campers were tired and already slipping into a natural routine.

From the far end of the mess hall came a clatter of dishes as Mrs. Hancock and her evening staff of helpers went about getting the meal under way. Ed glanced in their direction absently. He ought to go read the bulletin board to see whether or not he had been assigned evening or early-morning KP, but he didn't go. He was too relaxed and comfortable to move just now.

He saw Mr. Hancock leave the mess hall and start toward the group around the campfire and wondered why his usually smiling face looked so strangely solemn.

"Boys and girls," he said when he came up to the group. At first some of them did not hear and kept on talking, so he had to raise his voice a little. "Campers, have any of you been into the supplies this afternoon? The groceries?"

Everyone stopped what he was doing. Mr. Hancock waited a moment in the sudden silence, then went on.

"Quite a number of groceries have disappeared this afternoon. Whoever took them felt he was being honest, because a dollar bill was left in their place. We don't want anyone to be hungry, but we would prefer that you ask before you take anything. It's a little annoying when you're counting on certain things for a meal to find that they aren't there."

The campers looked at each other with blank faces.

"Well, never mind. We'll just forget about it this time," said Mr. Hancock understandingly. "I just hope that nothing else disappears around here. And I'm sure it won't. We've never had any trouble before."

"But it has, Mr. Hancock." Ed was a little surprised to hear his own voice. All of a sudden he was convinced that the disappearance of his sleeping bag was no joke. It was more serious than that. "My sleeping bag's gone. It was in my tent when we went swimming, but it isn't there now."

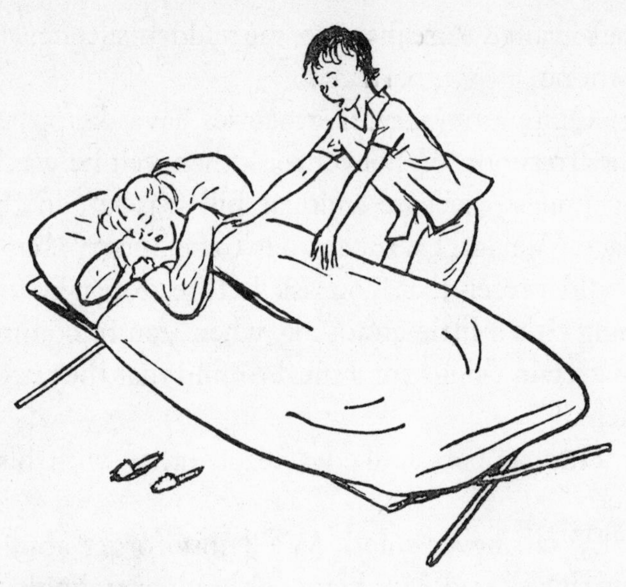

Eight

It seemed to Priscilla that she had barely closed her eyes when Ginny was shaking her awake.

"Hurry up," she said impatiently. "You're the last one up. It's the third time I've called you."

The six other girls who shared the tent with them were almost dressed. They were chattering away as easily as though they had been awake for hours, discussing their plans for the day. They were all older than she and Ginny and, while they were friendly enough, Priscilla still felt a little shy in their company.

"I'll only be a minute," she gasped, kicking herself loose from the sleeping bag. Ginny was already dressed, and Priscilla didn't want to be left alone with the others, particularly because of what had happened yesterday. Somehow she sensed that there was a little criticism about her dive off the bridge. Even those who had been free with their congratulations at first were a little more reserved now. Perhaps they believed as Ed did that she was a show-off, but she hadn't thought of it that way. They all knew a lot about science and she didn't. She had only been trying to prove that she excelled in something.

She was sure that Ed and his criticism were to blame for everything. He was horrible, dreadful, and she hoped he never did find his missing sleeping bag. He had certainly caused enough commotion in camp with that announcement yesterday. Things had been turned upside down in a search, but it hadn't been found. Probably, if the truth were known, he had hidden it himself just to get attention.

"We can come back after breakfast to straighten the tent," said Ginny. "We've got to be there for the flag raising."

Priscilla was sure she had never dressed so fast in her life. She jumped into her clothes, brushed madly at her pony tail, and tied it back without even a glance at the scrap of a mirror which one of the girls had thoughtfully hung in the tent. She washed her hands and face in the tin basin outside, not even stopping to think, as she had last night, that the water was cold, brushed her teeth, and managed to reach the flagpole just in time to see the Stars and Stripes begin the upward climb for the day.

"I just signed us in under the wire for the hike," confided Ginny at breakfast. "They don't like to take more than eight or nine in a group, and lots of people wanted to look for geodes this morning."

"Are they hard to find?"

"They're not easy. Especially good ones. Last year a boy found one that looked exactly like a crystal vase. It was about so high, and you'd have thought it came from a jewelry store. I'd sure like to find one like that, wouldn't you?"

"It would be nice," agreed Priscilla politely.

She still couldn't see why all these people were so interested in rocks. If they were looking for diamonds, or even for amethysts, such as Ed had in his collection, it might be different. Those things were valuable as jewelry.

When they had finished breakfast and tidied their tents, the campers each picked up a sack lunch and a canteen from the pile laid out on the mess-hall table and began gathering around their group leaders.

"Come on," said Ginny. "We go with Mr. Graves. He's over here."

Priscilla followed eagerly enough, but as they

approached the group she hesitated. How could she have forgotten that her cousin's primary interest was rocks? Of course he would have signed up for this trip, and there he was, right beside the leader.

Ed had managed to clean himself up a little since his return from swimming yesterday, although she had thought as she saw him jump off the truck that it would be an impossible undertaking. He was being as loud and as obnoxious as ever, for even from this distance she could hear him boasting about what he proposed to find on the day's field trip.

She wondered if it was too late to change her mind about going to the zeolite beds. Perhaps she would be better off with the fossil hunters, or it might be better to fall back on her nonexistent interest in botany. She would hate to have Ed think she was tagging along after him, and that's exactly what he would think. He had warned her against doing such a thing before they left home. Then she saw that it was too late to do anything, for Mr. Graves had seen them.

"Here come our other two," he called. "You girls make nine of us. Come on, let's get started."

Priscilla saw Ed scowl at her; then in the excitement of their departure, he seemed to forget all about her.

"It looks funny to see that patch of green stuff

over there," said Priscilla diffidently as they started out. Ginny hadn't been exactly cool since yesterday, but Priscilla couldn't help feeling that she wasn't quite so friendly as she had been before. "It looks like an oasis in the desert."

"That's the swamp," explained Ginny. "It's filled with little springs and things, and we aren't allowed inside the barbwire fence they've strung around it."

"Is it quicksand?" asked Priscilla respectfully.

"I don't know whether it's quicksand. It's probably all boggy mud though, and you'd sink down. There are lots of nettles in there growing with the reeds. And the rattlesnakes come down there to drink. At night after supper it's a good hike there and back. Just the right distance."

"I thought you weren't allowed to take hikes alone."

"You aren't. But you can walk there and back with somebody else. It's kind of fun. The swamp's full of frogs, and they're always squawking."

Priscilla looked at the swamp respectfully. They needn't worry about her wanting to break that rule. She didn't like frogs, and as for rattlesnakes, she'd go out of her way to avoid them.

"You know," said Ginny after a moment. "This is a funny camp. It's not like any other camp you ever heard of. There aren't very many rules, so everybody bends over backward about keeping them. You don't go inside the swamp, and you don't ever go on a hike alone, and you don't go outside the swimming hole boundaries, and now you don't dive off the bridge."

"If you mean me, I didn't break a rule," protested Priscilla. "It wasn't a rule when I did it, and anyway I landed inside the boundary."

"But you landed right on the edge, and now we have another rule," said Ginny ruefully.

Priscilla clamped her lips firmly together and said nothing. So that was what was the matter with everyone. They blamed her for the existence of a new rule. Well, there was nothing she could do about it now. She'd just have to wait and hope they would forget about it, but she certainly wished she had never come to this stupid camp in the first place.

As field trips were calculated at Camp Hancock, it wasn't a very long walk to the zeolite beds, and the early morning was pleasant. The sun had not yet climbed high enough to make things uncomfortably warm or to awaken the shimmering heat waves which would dance across the desertlike expanses in the afternoon. There was a clarity in the air which made it possible to see for miles and miles in every direction and brought into sharp focus every little stem and minute leaf on the sagebrush. In the west, three snow-capped mountains—Jefferson, Hood, and St. Helens—seemed to float

The zeolite beds were in a rocky canyon

gently in a pale blue sky. If you looked closely you could see that they were resting on a thin blue line, which was the lower range of the Cascades, only faintly visible above the monotonous stretch of brown plateau.

"Are they going to set off dynamite today?" asked Priscilla finally. She would just have to go along as though nothing had happened.

"No, they only do that in the nut beds," Ginny reminded her.

"Do we just go around looking for things the way we did yesterday?"

"And picking at them," nodded Ginny. "Oh, I forgot. You don't have a hammer, do you? We should have borrowed one from somebody."

"A hammer?"

"A geologist's hammer. It's pretty much like a regular one, only it's flat on one end so you can use it to break stones, and sharp on the other so you can use it for a chisel. Well, never mind," she decided cheerfully, "I've got a chisel in my pack, and we can share my hammer."

"I wouldn't want to take it away from you," said Priscilla quickly. "I'll just be poking around today anyway. I wouldn't know a geode if I saw one."

"Don't worry. You'll learn fast," Ginny reassured her.

The zeolite beds, where most of them hoped to

find geodes, were in a rocky canyon between two rimrock ledges. When the sun was higher in the sky, it would undoubtedly be flooded with heat, but now it was only pleasantly warm. The others began searching among the rocks, picking at one, then another, with their snub-nosed hammers, or cracking with their steel chisels. Priscilla pretended to search too, but she really wasn't interested in finding anything. Already she was beginning to wonder how long they would stay here. She knew she wouldn't be permitted to return to camp alone. That would be breaking a rule, and she certainly didn't intend to do that.

Ginny had completely forgotten to lend her the hammer or chisel, but it really didn't matter. She walked along slowly, her eyes on the ground, kicking at rocks and boulders with her toe. Suddenly her eye was caught by a gleam of something pink. In this vast stretch of gray and brown, it stood out as noticeably as a crocus in a green lawn. She reached over and picked it up.

It was a rock clearly enough, almost the size of her fist, but the pink portion was only part of it. Most of the rock was gray, like the cliff above her, and the pink seemed to continue inward a little way, as though it might be the filling inside a chocolate cream.

In spite of her disinterest in rocks, she felt a little glow of triumph. This must be a geode certainly, and one which had already been broken in half. Here were all these experienced rock hounds looking as hard as they could, and she had been the one to find it.

"Ginny!" she called in excitement. "I found one! I found one!"

Ginny stopped what she was doing and hurried over, and Mr. Graves, too, joined them. She held out her find for them to see, and Mr. Graves took it from her.

"Is it a geode?" she demanded.

Mr. Graves shook his head and held the rock so Ginny could see it too.

"I'm afraid not," he said. "But it's a good specimen just the same. Want to try a guess, Ginny?"

"It could be quartz," she decided after a minute. "Quartz is that shade of pink sometimes, but the shine isn't quite right. It's either feldspar, or maybe calcite."

"Why don't you test it, Priscilla?" suggested Mr. Graves. "Whichever it is, you'll want to save it for your collection, anyway."

"Test it?" she repeated vaguely.

"This is her first field trip, Mr. Graves," explained Ginny quickly. "She doesn't know anything about minerals yet."

"Then this is a good time to learn," decided Mr. Graves. "First of all, let's see if we can't dislodge it from the surrounding rock."

He went to work carefully with a knife and chisel. Much to Priscilla's surprise, the grayish rock was softer than it had first seemed to her touch. In a matter of minutes he had laid the pink center bare. It was only about the size of a walnut, not so large as she had expected it to be, and Ginny, too, was disappointed.

"I thought she'd found a great big hunk of it," she admitted.

"So did I," agreed Mr. Graves. "But this is a good size to use for testing. Here, Priscilla, take the hammer and hit your specimen as hard as you can."

It seemed like a silly thing to do, but she did as she was told. She balanced the pink stone on a large boulder and brought down the flat end of the hammer as hard as she could. She hadn't expected anything to happen, but she felt it crack beneath the blow. Mr. Graves smiled and picked up the pieces.

"Look at the break," he told her. "How many clean, flat surfaces did it make?"

"Three," she counted. The fragments looked even prettier now that she could see inside. While they were still predominantly pink, they now shone with rainbow colors; and when she held one to the light, it was almost transparent.

"It's calcite," decided Ginny proudly. "Calcite has cleavage in three directions. Feldspar only breaks clean in two. As soon as you got it out of the other rock I knew it couldn't be quartz, because the sides didn't meet at an angle."

"Sometimes feldspar breaks quite well in the third direction," objected Mr. Graves. "I've been fooled by it myself."

Priscilla looked at them blankly. She didn't have the slightest idea what they were talking about, and Mr. Graves must have realized it, for he hurried to explain.

"Quartz, feldspar, and calcite are all minerals, Priscilla. When people call us rock hounds, they aren't exactly right, because we are generally looking for minerals instead. Quartz and feldspar are probably the two most important minerals in the world, and they're found everywhere. We couldn't get along without them. Beach sand is mostly quartz and feldspar. Clay, from which dishes and bricks are made, comes from feldspar. Both of them are found in many kinds of rocks, and so is calcite. Calcite is the third most common mineral."

"But I've never seen anything like this before," Priscilla insisted.

"Have you ever seen stalactites? Or stalagmites? They're calcite. And little particles of it are found in many kinds of rocks. You just haven't given it a second glance."

"Well, is this feldspar or calcite?" demanded Ginny impatiently.

Mr. Graves smiled and reached into his pocket. He pulled out a handful of small change and handed Priscilla a penny.

"Rub this against your specimen and see what happens," he said. "You'll have to use pressure."

Priscilla rubbed the penny as hard as she could against one of the freshly broken sides of the pink mineral. When she took it away, there was a faint scratch on the specimen and another on the coin.

"I knew it," said Ginny in satisfaction. "It's calcite. They scratched each other. They're the same hardness. Metal won't scratch feldspar."

"Let's do one more test," grinned Mr. Graves. "You'll find a bottle of soda in my knapsack, Ginny."

Priscilla stared openmouthed as Ginny brought an unopened bottle of soda pop to the boulder beside which they were standing. Mr. Graves put one of the pink fragments in a little hollow of the gray rock, opened the pop, and poured some over the specimen. Instantly it fizzed and boiled up, like a minute volcano.

"That settles it," nodded Ginny. "Calcite always fizzes that way with soda. I'm going back to my geode hunting."

"I'm sorry this wasn't a geode, Priscilla," said Mr. Graves gently. "And I'm sorry, too, that this wasn't as large a specimen of calcite as we thought it would be. But perhaps you can find another."

"Oh, that's all right," she said quickly. "I've got lots of time to look."

After he had gone away, she went back to the boulder and, gathering up the pieces of pink mineral, put them in her pocket. Maybe they were small, as he and Ginny had said, but somehow she couldn't bear to throw them away.

Nine

"Mr. Graves! Mr. Graves! I've found something!"

Priscilla's voice rose shrilly above the pick-pick of steel hammers, and most of the group looked up. Only Ed kept his head bent diligently over his work.

This morning the rock hounds had come to one of the several agate beds, and as usual Ed had been more than a little upset when he saw that his cousin and Ginny were again signed up for the same group. Perhaps by this time he should be reconciled to their company, but he wasn't. Priscilla had no right to be here. He was here first, and she didn't even like rocks. She only pretended to. Maybe Mr. Graves was taken in by her mock interest. Probably he was, for Ed had seen the instructor give her some books on rocks last night at dinner. Priscilla had gushed and gooed in that sticky way of hers, and while the others were singing around the campfire, he had glimpsed her at one end of the mess table pretending to read. She may have fooled the others, but she didn't fool Ed, not one minute. She was just trying to impress people.

Now he went on working as though he hadn't heard her call out, picking away at the rocks with the sharp edge of his hammer, but her voice and that of the leader carried quite clearly, and he listened intently.

"Let's see, Priscilla," said Mr. Graves.

"I don't know what it is, exactly, but I'm sure it's something!" announced Priscilla excitedly.

Ed snorted to himself. That kind of a remark was a dead giveaway. It proved that she didn't know anything at all about rocks or minerals, or she at least would have hazarded a guess.

"I'm not just sure either, Priscilla," said Mr. Graves after a moment. "We'll have to take it back to camp and use the diamond saw on it. My guess is that it's a bit of petrified wood, but we've never found any at this spot before."

"Petrified wood!" gasped Priscilla. "That's wood that's turned into stone, isn't it?"

"Not exactly," corrected Mr. Graves. "The wood cells and fibers have been replaced by stone. Petrified wood is usually some form of quartz—

agate, jasper, sometimes opal. When a tree fell into water, silica seeped into the cells and created the change. There's no wood fiber left here at all."

"Then it's a real specimen!" cried Priscilla. "A mineral specimen!"

At least her reading had taught her not to call a mineral a rock, thought Ed sourly. She'd learned that much, anyway. He wished that he had been the one to find the piece of petrified wood. He didn't have one in his collection as yet. But then, they weren't too hard to find, he told himself quickly, or he could always trade for one. He probably could have several by the time he went home, if he wanted to bother looking. He went on doggedly, tapping, picking, prying.

"Boy, it's sure hot today," observed Duane, coming up beside him. He wiped his face with his handkerchief, leaving a dirty smear across each cheek. "Have you had any luck yet?"

"I've found a couple that I'm going to take back to camp and polish up," Ed told him, glad of the chance to straighten up and rest a moment. "They're agate all right, but they may not be much good."

"Me too," said Duane gloomily. "Seems to me I had better luck last year. Anyway, I don't remember it's ever being this hot."

"The trouble with this place is that it's too crowded," said Ed, glaring over his shoulder.

"There are only nine of us," protested Duane. "Ten, counting Mr. Graves."

"It's still too crowded to do any real hunting. Especially in a picked-over bed."

"How can you say it's picked over?" protested Duane. "There are—"

"Just the same," interrupted Ed quickly, "let's scout around and find a new spot. Just the two of

"The trouble with this place is that it's too crowded."

us. This place makes me sick."

"Well, I suppose we might find one if we're lucky," admitted Duane. He brightened with a sudden idea. "Let's go up to the Shepherd's Cabin! It's not too far from here. Let's ask Mr. Graves right now."

The leader agreed, after a little persuasion, that they could go by themselves.

"Only don't get lost," he warned. "Don't try to go any farther than the cabin, and if you want to go swimming with us this afternoon be sure you're back at camp by three."

It was exciting, being off on their own. Last year they hadn't been allowed to do so, since they were the youngest campers and it was their first experience at Camp Hancock. Now they were old hands, and it was all right to venture off in pairs. They started out, knapsacks hanging from their shoulders. The sun no longer seemed to burn with such a sizzling vengeance but cast a benign beam on what might well turn out to be an adventure. They saw no new places likely to yield geological treasure, but that was no great disappointment. They had known before they started that they wouldn't do that.

"Do you know what would be a good thing to have up here?" said Duane after a while. "A helicopter. It would save a lot of climbing up and down."

"It sure would. Those agate beds wouldn't be more than a mile and a half from camp by air."

"But I bet we walked three miles going around cliffs to get there, and it's another mile up to the cabin."

"Oh, maybe not that much," objected Ed. "What's the matter? You getting tired?"

"Oh no," objected Duane quickly. "Just hungry. And I could use a drink. But I think I'll wait till we get to the spring. The water in my canteen's warm by this time."

"It won't be long now," encouraged Ed. "We'll eat as soon as we get there."

The Shepherd's Cabin, long deserted by the original resident, was a one-room shack set in the midst of nowhere. Years before, when sheep had grazed the spring grass of the surrounding range lands, it had been used regularly, but now it sheltered only a very rare overnight tenant. It was most easily reached by a rutty dirt road which meandered off from the highway near the small town of Clarno and petered out at the cabin itself. Picnic parties occasionally visited the spot, for there was a spring of fresh water, but the campers from Hancock were its most enthusiastic visitors.

Every summer they brought a few nails and tightened loose boards in the cabin, swept the creaky, splintering floor with the moldy broom which was one of the fixtures of the place, and sometimes built a juniper-wood fire in the rusty contrivance which passed for a stove.

"I bet we're the first ones here this year," gloated Ed as they came in sight of the sagging structure.

One had to look carefully to see the cabin itself,

"If you had to hide out, this would be the place to come."

for it was weathered almost to the shade of the surrounding land. More evident to the eye was the splotch of green bushes and straggling grass growing beside the spring.

"No," argued Duane. "The kids from the first session must have come up here. Come on. I'll race you."

They tore over the rough ground, which tried to trip their feet, their knapsacks pounding and slapping at their sweating backs. Duane won, as he always did, because his legs were longer; and he threw himself, panting, on the single wobbly step which led to the front door.

"Boy," gasped Ed, avoiding the subject of who had won the race. "Isn't this a swell hide-out? I wish I could live here all the time."

"I won," Duane reminded him automatically. He turned his head and looked up at the splintered gray building. "I don't think I'd like it all the time, but if you had to hide out this would be the place to come. They'd never think to look for you here."

"Maybe at the end of the session, when the others go back to town, you and I could bring our sleeping bags up here and stay awhile," suggested Ed. "It would sure be fun, if our folks would let us."

"They wouldn't," said Duane practically. "And anyway, you don't have a sleeping bag any more. That blanket Mrs. Hancock lent you wouldn't be enough if it was really cold. You still haven't found yours. Let's go see if the spring's been cleared out."

The spring was always something of a miracle to Ed. It wasn't the sort that bubbled from the ground—at least one couldn't see that it bubbled. The water just seemed to appear. It formed an oblong pool, perhaps three feet across, and the surrounding earth was damp and oozy for a distance of another foot. It seemed strange to find a spring of this kind in a desertlike stretch, and every time he came here he couldn't help wondering if it might not have disappeared since the last time. Today the thought came to him again, for Duane, in the lead, gave an exclamation of surprise.

"Ed! Look!"

"What's the matter? What's wrong?" He hurried, expecting as always to find that the water was gone and that there was only a circle of saffron sand. He was surprised to see that the spring was just as it had been before.

"What's eating you, anyway?" he demanded.

"There!" pointed Duane dramatically. "Right at the edge of the spring, on the other side."

Ed leaned over and squinted in the direction of the pointing finger.

"It's a hoofmark! Looks like a horse."

"Certainly it's a horse," agreed Duane. "But what's a horse doing here? There's no ranch for miles and miles, and anyway, ranches use jeeps these days."

"Just the same, a horse stood right there and drank out of the spring."

"Oh well," Duane lost interest and shrugged the whole thing off. "So what?"

"I'll tell you what," said Ed in excitement. "Maybe it's a wild horse. And maybe we could capture it and take it home."

"I never heard of any wild horses around here. And anyway, don't they always run in herds? Only one horse has been here."

"Herds have to get started someway," pointed out Ed sensibly. "They have to build up. Besides, maybe this is the scout for the herd, out looking for water."

"It could be," agreed Duane doubtfully.

"And if we keep our eyes open and carry a rope wherever we go, we might be able to capture it."

"You carry the rope," scoffed Duane. "Let's have our drink, then go inside and look around."

They leaned over the spring, scooping up handfuls of water to drink. The ground surrounding the water was so soft that the soles of their shoes sank well into the mud. It felt cool and soothing against their hot feet.

"Had enough?" demanded Ed finally; and when Duane nodded, "Let's not fill our canteens again till we get ready to go back. It will stay cooler that way."

The cabin door squeaked and cried out in both rusty hinges when they pushed it open and stepped inside. After the bright sunlight, it was so dark that they blinked from sudden blindness.

"It doesn't smell all shut up the way it usually does," said Ed in surprise.

"Course not. The campers from the last session probably gave it a good airing," Duane reminded him. "They should have oiled those hinges on the door, though."

By this time their eyes were growing accustomed to the change, and they were beginning to see. Everything was just as they expected. There was the battered old stove, one leg propped up with a stick of wood, its top and sides red with rust. There were two chairs, both missing rungs and one without any back, a rough table nailed together by someone who hadn't been much of a carpenter, and in the corner a boxlike affair which could serve as a bed. When their eyes reached the bed, they stopped, widening with astonishment.

Today the old straw which ordinarily filled the box and served as a mattress was not in evidence. It was neatly concealed by a khaki-colored sleeping bag. After a long moment Ed advanced cautiously and turned down one side of the bag.

"It's mine," he announced in an awe-struck tone. "It's the one that was stolen!"

"Are you sure?" demanded Duane.

"Sure, I'm sure. Those are my blankets inside with my name on. And look at this stain. That's mustard. It came from a hot dog."

"But how'd it get up here?"

"Somebody carried it," said Ed grimly. "Somebody who rides a horse and who has been using this cabin for a hide-out. I think we'd better get back to camp and tell Mr. Hancock to call the sheriff. I think a desperado has been holing up here —maybe a bank robber—and he's been using my sleeping bag too."

Ten

"I'd just as soon not go swimming today," Priscilla told Mr. Graves as they started back from their field trip. She could hardly wait to polish her specimen of petrified wood. "If you'd show me how, I'll do the cutting and polishing while the rest of you go to the river."

"It's up to you," Mr. Graves assured her, smiling in sympathy. "You can stay and work if you'd rather. I don't blame you, either. I think you've got something there. Mr. Hancock will be really excited if you've found petrified wood in those agate beds."

The two boys were beginning the story of their adventure all over again

But when they reached camp, Mr. Hancock was not there. He had gone to town for the sheriff, and everyone was jumping up and down with excitement.

"What is it?" demanded Ginny. "What's happened?"

"Bandits!" someone told her. "Ed Herrick and Duane Carpenter went up to the Shepherd's Cabin. They found a real gangster hangout. I guess they were lucky to get away at all."

"Criminy!" exclaimed Ginny with shining eyes. "Where are they?"

"Did they get wounded?" asked Priscilla anxiously. Of course it didn't really matter to her if Ed was hurt, but Aunt Margaret would feel dreadful about it.

"They're over there, in the mess hall. They're telling everybody all about it."

"Come on," shrieked Ginny, but Priscilla had already started.

Ed and Duane were standing at one end of the table, on top of which was the khaki-covered sleeping bag. About them was a great crowd of campers, which was being constantly added to as the various expeditions returned from their field trips. The two boys were beginning the story of their adventure all over again; and, although it was not the first time some of the campers had heard it, no one made a move to leave.

"Well, we got there, see," Ed was saying, "and the first thing we saw was a hoofmark in the mud by the spring."

"I spotted it first," Duane reminded him.

"Sure, but you didn't think it amounted to anything. I knew the minute I saw it something was up," insisted Ed. "It shouldn't have been there. It's miles from a ranch, and the way they use jeeps nowadays . . ."

"Well, anyway, we went inside," interrupted Duane hastily. "And it didn't smell shut up, like it generally does. Somebody'd been using that cabin. We knew it the minute we opened the door."

"And there was my bedroll, all spread out as nice as you please! The nerve of them, coming into camp here and swiping my bedroll and taking it up there to sleep in!"

"And there were orange peelings in the stove, too," said Duane. "Fresh ones! Whoever ate that orange must have done it this morning or last night."

"Did you find anything else?"

"We didn't have time. We didn't want to give the desperado time to get away. We just took my bedroll and high-tailed it back here for the sheriff."

"Who do you suppose it is?" demanded someone in a frightened voice.

"Somebody that's wanted by the police," said

Ed positively. "That's a perfect hide-out up there. Duane and I were just talking about it. Maybe there's a reward for him too. Probably there is, and Duane and I will be rich."

"I don't see how you could expect to get it?"

"Why not?" demanded Ed and Duane in a single voice. "We reported it."

"Sure, and tipped off your hand by taking that bedroll. You should have left it there."

"It was my bedroll," muttered Ed ruefully. Obviously he hadn't thought of that.

"Just the same, it was pretty smart of you," said Ginny. "Finding it and all."

"I guess it must have been a hunch, going up to the cabin," agreed Ed. "And it sure paid off. The minute I saw the hoofmark, I knew something was up. I hope it's a real public enemy."

"They'll put our pictures in the paper if it is," said Duane. "And pictures of the camp, too."

The campers smiled. They wouldn't mind having their pictures in the paper.

"How'd you happen to go up there today?" asked someone curiously.

"Like I said, it was a hunch," answered Ed promptly. "Things haven't seemed just right around here, have they, Duane? And we thought we ought to have a little look around. So we went up to the cabin. At first everything seemed to be okay, then we saw that hoofprint in the spring . . ."

"I spotted it," said Duane.

Priscilla turned and walked away. Now that she knew that Ed hadn't been hurt and that Aunt Margaret would have no cause for worry, she didn't want to stay there any longer. She had never seen such a disgusting exhibition in her life. How dared he accuse her of being a show-off at the swimming hole? At least she had something to display, her skill as a swimmer. All Ed had done was stumble over a missing sleeping bag, and the way he was carrying on you'd think it was the most wonderful thing that ever happened.

She wandered over to the empty tent which was used as a workshop. Everyone was hanging around Ed and Duane, listening to them brag. Even Mr. Graves and the other leaders must be listening. Anyway, they weren't in here attending to serious matters like polishing a rare piece of petrified wood.

She took the specimen from her pocket and turned it over thoughtfully. If only she were a little more experienced, she would start on it herself, but she was afraid. She didn't even know how to begin. She wandered around looking at the various specimens on display in the tent. They were interesting to her now. They weren't just a collection of rocks.

From time to time she raised the tent flap and looked at the group still collected in the mess hall.

She didn't see how they could stand to hear the same story over and over. Probably there was nothing to it, anyway. Probably Ed had just made the whole thing up to get a little attention. It was quite possible that he had hidden his own sleeping bag and had managed to get it up to the cabin someway. She wouldn't put such a thing past him.

And yet—suppose he hadn't? Suppose there was a bandit lurking in the vicinity, waiting to swoop down on them at any moment? It happened in TV westerns, and there must be some basis of fact in them.

It made her a little uncomfortable to think of such things, and she was relieved when she heard a truck drive up outside, followed by a car. She opened the tent flap and looked out again. Mr. Hancock had returned in the truck, and the sheriff and another man had followed him in a jeep. The crowd over in the mess hall surged forward to meet them, and she observed scornfully how everyone fell back to let Ed and Duane lead the way. It was their moment, and they were certainly making the most of it.

The sheriff stayed only a little while. Then he and the other man got into their jeep and drove away, across country this time, toward the agate beds and the Shepherd's Cabin beyond.

"I think the best thing for us to do is to go swimming as usual," called Mr. Hancock. "By the time we're back, maybe the sheriff will have returned."

Priscilla put down the specimen which she hoped would be petrified wood, and started to get her suit. She might as well go. Everyone else was too stirred up to think of minerals this afternoon. Besides, if there was a bandit loose somewhere, it would be just as well to stay with the crowd.

Duane and Ed continued to be the center of attraction all afternoon. They went over their story a few more times, both going and coming in the truck, and the fact that it was of sufficient importance to call the sheriff out of his office added to their prestige.

"He should have taken us with him to the cabin," they added more than once. "We could have helped a lot."

Only Priscilla seemed to question the value of their presence when the sheriff revisited the cabin, and she was afraid to say anything. But even she was a little surprised to find that the sheriff had returned to camp before they did and was waiting for them. It certainly hadn't taken him very long to complete his investigation.

"Did you find them?" demanded Ed, pushing forward.

"Not a thing," said the sheriff. "We drove all over, too. There's no sign of anybody around there now."

"But somebody must have been there," said Mr. Hancock. "A sleeping bag can't walk away by itself."

"The way we've got it figured it's a tramp, a hobo," explained the sheriff. "Likely somebody who'd been through here before and knew about the cabin. He must have walked into your camp the day you all cleared out, and lifted the bag then. I wouldn't leave things unguarded again, if I were you."

"We won't," promised Mr. Hancock.

"Anyway, he took the bag, figuring it would be useful, but he hadn't counted on its being so heavy."

"It wasn't heavy," objected Duane. "It was light."

"It might seem heavy to a hobo. They travel even lighter than that," said the sheriff, his eyes twinkling. "Anyway, he decided not to bother with it, so he left it and went on."

"How about the orange peelings in the stove? Those were fresh," insisted Duane.

"They wouldn't dry up too quick shut up in there."

"And the horse's hoofprint," cried Ed. "How do you explain that?"

"I don't," said the sheriff. "But I don't think it means much. There are plenty of horses in the country. Maybe one got out of a corral somewhere and took a jaunt for himself before he went home."

"How about the groceries that disappeared?" asked Mrs. Hancock.

"Hobos don't leave dollar bills to pay for them, and neither do bandits," said the sheriff, grinning at Ed. "I think you can solve that one closer to home. Of course a passing hobo is just a theory, but it's the only one that comes to me right now. I'm certain of one thing, though. There's nobody up around there now, or we'd have seen him. Of course we'll keep our eyes open, and I don't think you ought to let the kids hike out alone. But they shouldn't do that anyway. It's too easy to get lost around here."

"We know," said Mr. Hancock. "I know they'll all be very careful about that."

Eleven

As Priscilla sealed the envelope of the short note she had scrawled to her mother, she realized it was unnaturally still outside. Only a moment before it had been so noisy she could hardly concentrate. She had deliberately made herself ignore the voices. Even when Ginny had opened the tent flap and called that everyone was collecting for the field trips, she had answered impatiently.

"You know they won't wait," warned Ginny pointedly. "And if you aren't there, you can't go by yourself. That's breaking a rule."

"I'm not going to break any rules," Priscilla muttered angrily. "Just go on."

This was the first time Ginny had mentioned rules since the walk to the zeolite beds, and Priscilla had begun to think she had been forgiven for causing a new one. Gradually the reserve of the other campers had relaxed, and she was being treated like everyone else. Certainly she wasn't going to do anything to jeopardize her present standing, but she did have to get this note finished and ready for the truck to take to the post office at Fossil.

They had been at Camp Hancock a week, and this was the first moment she had found to write her mother. While the others were writing letters, Priscilla had been reading the books on rocks and minerals which Mr. Graves had lent her. At first she hadn't meant to do much more than glance through them, but before she knew it she was reading every page. It had occupied all her spare time.

She licked a stamp, glued it on her letter, and dashed out of the tent into the freshness of the early morning. The flag atop the tall pole stirred ever so gently, hinting at a breeze which Priscilla could not feel, but there was no other movement in camp. They had gone on without her.

She walked over to the mess hall. On the long table was one paper bag, her own lunch. The end of the building containing the kitchen was deserted too this morning. Mrs. Hancock, who did not always accompany the campers on their expeditions, must have walked over to visit with one of the wives of the instructors who occupied a small tent city of their own a little behind the regular camp.

She would not be far away, for the kitchen and supplies were no longer being left unattended. Last night there had been another disappearance of food, and once again a dollar bill had been left in its place.

Priscilla put her letter with the stack waiting to be mailed, and sat down on one of the benches. She didn't quite know what to do next, and she felt a great resentment toward the others for not waiting. After all, it wasn't her fault she had to finish a letter. It wouldn't have hurt them to wait one minute; she certainly hadn't been any longer than that. Still, as she looked around and saw no distant figures in any direction, she had to admit that she might have been a little longer than one minute. Well, two minutes, then, she admitted, frowning. Then she remembered that today the largest party had signed up to visit the old mammal beds, which lay across the river. The distance was too far for walking, so they were using the larger truck. It wouldn't take a truck long to get out of sight.

She herself had signed up for that trip, not because she was particularly interested in fossils, but because Ginny was going. If it hadn't been for Ginny, she would have joined the smaller group returning to the agate beds. It would have been wonderful to dig out another piece of petrified wood as she had the last time.

That had been a real find. Both Mr. Graves and Mr. Hancock had said so, for it was their first piece of evidence of vegetation in that spot. When they sawed it open, it was tannish in color and looked like a piece of planed wood, only it didn't feel like wood. Moreover, there were no rings, which meant that it lived in an era of no seasons, that it underwent no periods of growth and dormancy.

Priscilla had been very excited. When she held it in her hand and they told her it was mineral, a form of quartz, she forgot all the disparaging things she had said to Ed about rocks. She wanted to know everything about them at once, to add to the discoveries she had already made. That's why she had been studying the books so hard.

She glared at the nearest rimrock cliff, behind which the small party destined for the agate beds must have just disappeared. They couldn't possibly have got any farther than there. If she hurried, she could overtake them. She had been there once, and she was sure she remembered the way.

She knew she ought to tell Mrs. Hancock that she was going, but if she took the time she would be left too far behind. Besides, Mrs. Hancock might not even know that she hadn't gone with the others, and if she found out she might say Priscilla was too late. She wasn't too late, for she was sure she could overtake them. She picked up the lunch, and with a swift glance over her shoulder to make sure she was unobserved she started out.

Ordinarily it was cool as they set out from camp in the early morning, but by the time she had reached the cliff she was damp with perspiration. Perhaps it was because she had run all the way. Certainly she was completely out of breath, and her throat was so dry she could hardly swallow. She had forgotten to bring a canteen of water, but in the paper lunch sack there would undoubtedly be a small can of tomato or grape juice. Because she was so thirsty, it seemed logical to drink it now. Someone would share his canteen with her at noon.

Opening the can took a little time, and when she finally rounded the cliff, the party bound for the agate beds was still out of sight. It didn't matter too much, for she knew where they were going.

This time she didn't race at full speed. She walked along briskly, but not fast enough to become breathless. Perhaps when she reached the agate beds no one would notice her arrival, and she could pretend she had been there all the time.

She was glad she had decided to overtake the others and not waste the whole day doing nothing in camp. She had finished the books, and she should be putting her knowledge to practical use.

She turned her newly educated eyes toward the low rolling Red Hills to the west. They seemed almost maroon this morning, and she nodded wisely, recalling that the color was caused by the presence of iron in the sedimentary rock. It must be the way the sunlight struck them, for they seemed closer than they had on her first trip to the agate beds.

She trudged on and on, over arid land which was all very much alike, skirting clumps of sagebrush, all of which grew in a very similar way, now and then hopping over boulders which certainly didn't look exactly like sedimentary rock and might possibly be the original magma from the earth's center, she decided. Now and then she circled small rises in the land which she remembered perfectly as being the ones the party had circled before, but for some reason or other the agate beds and the rock party did not appear in view.

The first inkling she had that she was lost came with the realization that the sun had been steadily climbing in the sky. By the time it was this high, they had been at the agate beds for some time. The only sensible thing to do was to climb to higher ground and look down. Perhaps in this way she could see the others.

It was some distance to the first sizable cliff of rimrock, and when she reached there the sun was even higher. In another hour it would be directly overhead. Scrambling up the cliff itself was not easy, either. When she reached the top, her knee stung where she had scraped it on a rock, and she was covered with dirt. She stood and looked around in every direction.

To the west were the Red Hills, with the three snowcaps resting above the blue Cascades; to the north was the conelike peak which someone had told her was Iron Mountain; to the east and south was rolling gray land studded with rimrock. She couldn't see the agate beds anywhere. She couldn't even see Camp Hancock.

Priscilla had never felt so lost and frightened in her life. The worst of it was, the whole thing was her own fault. She had broken a rule, even though she hadn't meant to at all. She had been sure she could overtake the others, but she hadn't; and now she had ended up on a hike by herself.

She sat down on the ground hopelessly. The sun beat down on her head, but she didn't even feel it. How long would it be before they found her she wondered. Perhaps they wouldn't find her at all. Perhaps they'd just go round and round, as she had done, and she would finally die of starvation. Tears of self-pity filled her eyes. They ran down her dirty cheeks, and before she knew it she was sobbing aloud.

She cried for some time, since there was no one to see her. For some reason it made her feel better to cry. The sobs were company in the lonely vastness of the place. After a while the tears stopped, but she still continued the moaning sound as a

"Ug!" said a voice. "Squaw big crybaby!"

matter of course. Suddenly, without warning, she heard a noise behind her.

"Ug!" said a voice. "Squaw big crybaby!"

She whirled around to see a boy about her own age who was regarding her with very evident disgust. He was not like the boys at home, nor the boys she had met at camp. He was not even like her cousin Ed. His only garment was a pair of brown pants which had been cut into fringe above a pair of beaded moccasins. His bare chest and arms were brown, and in his black hair he wore a single feather, kept in place by a rag wound around his forehead. A streak of red paint slashed down either cheek, and three black streaks ran from his lower lip to his chin.

"Who are you?" she gasped in amazement. "Are you an Indian?"

He nodded gravely, and the disgust he had shown at her weakness of tears was dissolved in his satisfaction at being recognized for what he was. After a moment he came and squatted beside her.

"Me Many Horse," he announced. "Great-great-grandson of Chief Many Horse of Tyigh tribe. Own much land. All land you see. Farther than you can ride in ten days."

"My!" said Priscilla, greatly impressed. "I didn't know there were any Indians around here. My cousin Ed said——"

"Huh!" said Many Horse in a tone which silenced further discussion on the subject. After a moment he looked suggestively at the battered sack of lunch which she had dropped down beside her. "Squaw got food?"

"Yes," said Priscilla quickly, reaching for the sack, and suddenly realizing she was hungry herself.

"You give Many Horse," he demanded, holding out his hand. "Brave eat first. Squaw last."

She handed him the sack meekly, recalling as she did so that she had read of this Indian custom of women waiting for the second table. However, it was such a relief to be found that she didn't resent watching him unwrap the sandwiches without offering her one. He would probably take her to the reservations—she had read that nowadays Indians lived on reservations—and she would ask the white agent to return her to Camp Hancock.

"That's peanut butter," she said politely, watching him bite into the sandwich and make a grimace of distaste. "I'm afraid the bread is dry. It always is up here, because of the humidity."

"Many Horse not like peanut butter," grunted the Indian, but he finished the half just the same. She watched him put the other half of sandwich to one side, hardly daring to hope it was for her, and unwrap the wax paper around the pickles. "Pop?" he demanded. "Squaw got pop?"

"No, no pop," she told him without surprise.

Naturally a modern Indian would know about soda pop. You read about the old ones asking for firewater, but of course that was before pop had been invented. "There was some grape juice, but I drank it."

"Ug," sneered Many Horse.

"Look," she said, "could you take me back to the camp? I'm lost. It's the place with all the tents—the tepees. There are lots of children there, about our age."

"Paleface camp," he scowled. Then he added curiously, "What do they do there? What do they look for every day?"

"Oh, you do know where it is then," she cried in delight; then, as she saw his scowl deepen fiercely, she hurried to answer his question. "They look for things to do with science. Of course you don't know what that is. Things about nature. Fossils and rocks and minerals. And they study wildlife and things. At night they look through a big, big tube. That's called a telescope, and they're looking at the stars. Will you take me there?"

"What you give Many Horse to take you there?" he demanded after a moment.

"Why—why, I haven't got anything," she stammered. "At least I don't think I have. What do you want?" She racked her brains trying to remember any items she had read about which were usually carried by Indian traders. She couldn't think of any but beads, and she had none of those, even at camp.

"Food," he said promptly. "You bring food every night to a place Many Horse show you. And you promise to tell nobody you see Many Horse. Paleface not know him here."

"I'm not sure I can get food," she hesitated. "Oh, I can buy candy at the canteen, I suppose. And if somebody goes into Fossil, maybe I could have them buy me cookies or fruit. I can't get regular food out of the kitchen, though."

"No food, Many Horse leave squaw here," he said flatly.

She was filled with sudden panic at the thought of being deserted.

"I promise," she said quickly. "I'll do whatever you say. I won't tell a soul that I met you. And I'll bring food–somehow–every night. Only it will have to be a place close to camp. I can't go very far. It's against the rules to go out alone."

"Ug." He accepted her word and offered her the remaining half sandwich, getting to his feet at the same time. "You come. Many Horse take squaw back."

She followed him as fast as she could, nibbling at the dry sandwich as she went. Many Horse was obviously at home in this terrain, for his moccasined feet sped over the rough ground. Soon they came to a place where three gnarled juniper trees grew closely together. The ground dropped off a foot or two below them, and in this hollow stood a black and white pony.

"A horse!" cried Priscilla in delight. "Oh, the sweet thing."

"Stand back," warned Many Horse quickly. "Him wild Indian pony. Not used to squaws."

But he spoke too late. Priscilla had already rushed forward and was running her hand over the horse's head. The wild Indian pony nickered gently and rubbed his nose against her hand.

"What's his name?" she demanded.

"Lightning Bolt," scowled Many Horse.

"He must be fast," she said admiringly.

"Him very fast," agreed Many Horse, his frown relaxing a little. "Faster than the wind."

He untied the rope by which Lightning Bolt had been secured to one of the junipers, rolled it neatly, and fastened it on the saddle. Then, scorning the stirrup, he leaped into the saddle.

"Could I ride too?" asked Priscilla meekly. "I'm awfully tired, and it's so hot."

Many Horse's painted face wrinkled for a moment, but he gave in.

"Get on," he said gruffly.

She scrambled up behind him, and Lightning Bolt started off. He, too, must have felt the sun, for his progress gave no hint of the speed his owner had boasted for him. Priscilla was not critical. She was too relieved to be headed back toward camp, and it was nice to be on a horse once more. Next to swimming, riding was her favorite sport, although she doubted that an Indian pony, if Lightning Bolt was a good example, would be greatly prized in any of the riding academies at home.

"Why, there's the swamp!" she cried suddenly, sighting a splotch of green ahead. "I know where we are now. I could probably find my way from here."

"Squaw hush up," said Many Horse. "Sit still."

Lightning Bolt plodded forward, and Priscilla strained her eyes, looking for the familiar tents. They were not to be seen. The swamp, too, looked strange, and she made up her mind that it was a different swamp from the one close to Camp Hancock. In a few moments Many Horse pulled his pony to a standstill.

"Lightning Bolt stay here," he announced. "Black and white pony easy to see. Many Horse and squaw walk."

Obediently Priscilla climbed down after him. She gave Lightning Bolt one last affectionate pat before she fell in behind the small Indian. They seemed to be traveling along a little dry gulch, for on either side the ground sloped up for the distance of a foot or two. A moment later Many Horse crouched down, although he continued to move forward in the gully. Since he motioned her to do the same, Priscilla followed as best she could, but it was such an awkward position and made her feel so silly that she had to stifle a giggle.

Presently Many Horse stopped.

"Here," he whispered. "This spot. Every night squaw bring food. Leave here. Remember promise."

"But the camp," she protested. "You said you'd take me back to the camp."

"Camp there," he said impatiently. "Stand up. Squaw see."

She raised herself to her full height. They had completely circled the swamp, and it now lay at her left. She hadn't recognized it before because they were passing the opposite side, which faced the camp. It was familiar enough now. Straight ahead, dozing in the afternoon sun, were the tents of Camp Hancock.

Twelve

All the way to the old mammal beds that morning Ed kept his eyes open for a possible herd of wild horses. Of course if he could actually capture one it would be best of all, but he would even settle on being the first to sight such an unlikely phenomenon, since everyone agreed there were no such herds in this part of the state. Wild horses seemed the only thing left to him since the sheriff had calmly shattered his theory of bandits hiding in the rimrock.

Ed had thoroughly enjoyed his hours of being a celebrity, and he couldn't understand Duane at all for giving them up so easily. Duane seemed perfectly willing to forget all the glory which might have been theirs. He seemed to think it was enough that they had recovered the sleeping bag, and he had joined the others in kidding Ed about possible fleas which the tramp might have left behind in the blankets. Fortunately there were no fleas. At least the tramp had been clean.

By this morning everyone but Ed had put the whole thing in the back of his mind. They were much more concerned with the fact that four bags of lunch, prepared for the next day, had been taken from the kitchen during the night and a dollar bill left in their place.

Ed had suggested hopefully that the tramp might be hanging around after all, but everyone reminded him that a tramp wouldn't leave a dollar bill, and he had to admit they were right. After all, no money had been left for the sleeping bag. These two incidents were probably not connected, but he refused to give up the hoofprint that easily. No matter what the sheriff said, it could belong to a wild horse. Ed wasn't going to say anything to anybody, though. He'd just wait and watch, and if he were right he would have all the glory himself.

He came to with a start, realizing that Duane had just spoken to him.

"You don't suppose they'll call in the sheriff about those missing lunches?" repeated Duane in a low voice. "They were sure upset."

"I don't blame them," said Ed. "It was a sneaky thing to do."

"I know it. And the worst of it is, the sheriff

thinks it's one of us. He's already as much as said so. I don't know how he'd go about proving who it was, though."

"Oh, they've got ways," Ed reminded him. "They'd set a trap. First of all, he'd get everybody all calmed down and unsuspicious. They don't ever want to start a panic, you know. They want everything just as it is normally——" His mouth fell open in surprise. What a fool he had been! He, who knew all the tricks of western heroes, to say nothing of TV detectives! Why, it was exactly what the sheriff was doing right now. He was deliberately throwing everybody off guard with his suggested theory about the tramp. Naturally the sheriff wouldn't want the campers to show signs of alarm or nervousness while he was conducting his investigations.

Dreams of wild horses rapidly faded from his mind as he mulled over the possibilities of this greater claim to glory, for it was his claim. He was the one who had put the sheriff on the track.

He continued to think about it when they arrived at the old mammal beds, all the while Mr. Hancock was explaining them to the new campers.

"A paleontologist expects to find things in layers," said Mr. Hancock. "The newest things are on top, the oldest on the bottom, because that's the way they were built, layer upon layer. At the bottom we can expect to find shell fossils, sea

dinosaurs, ammonites. We've found some ammonites around here as big as the steering wheels of cars. Those go back to the Cretaceous era, seventy-five to a hundred million years ago. The layer above that is the Eocene era, fifty to sixty million years ago. In that layer are plants. Our nut beds belong to that age . . ."

Ed's scurrying thoughts drove the sound of Mr. Hancock's voice from his mind. He had been right in the beginning. This was the way people conducting investigations always acted. They gave out a glib and easy story for the public, but they didn't believe it themselves, not for one minute. How stupid he was for allowing himself to be dissuaded so easily.

"From the Miocene era we've found fossil remains of mastodons, small rhinos, the little three-

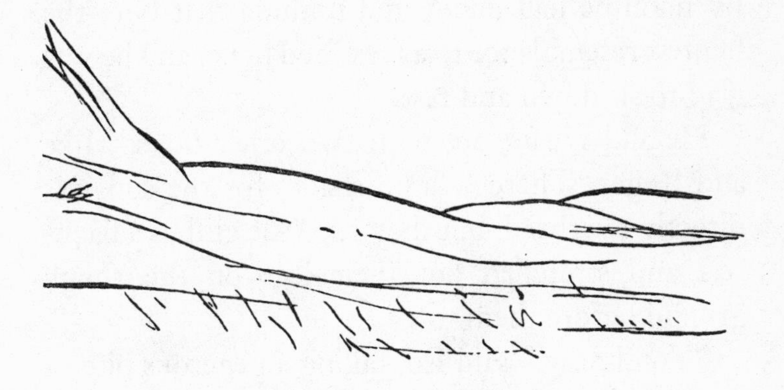

Dreams of wild horses rapidly faded from Ed's mind

toed horse, and so on, in these parts," said Mr. Hancock. "And today you may discover something entirely new, something we've never believed until now lived around here. Good luck to you."

The campers advanced enthusiastically on the cliff; and Ed, coming to with a start, hurried to select what seemed to be a likely spot for himself. Temporarily the prospects of excavation drove the thoughts of a desperado from his mind. It would be nice to find a dinosaur bone, and it was enough of a challenge to drag him away from rocks for one day, particularly when a long truck trip was involved.

He checked the spot he had chosen with Mr. Hancock to see that it met with the approval of an expert, and began chipping away at the cliff. It was slow work and, for him, not very rewarding. By noon he had uncovered nothing that bore the faintest resemblance to a fossilized bone, and he was glad to sit down and rest.

He and Duane ate with two other boys, Mike and Roger. There was no shade, for the sun was directly overhead, but they used the cliff as a backrest and stretched out their legs on the rough ground before them.

"You know," said Ed, taking a generous bite of sandwich, "I've been thinking. I don't believe it was a tramp who stole my sleeping bag."

"Who do you think it was then?" asked Duane in surprise.

"I think it was a criminal. A desperado hiding out. And I think the sheriff knows it, too, only he doesn't want us to get all scared and panicky about it."

"Then why didn't he come back with a posse and smoke him out?" demanded Mike. "If it was a real criminal, the sheriff wouldn't have just gone back to town the way he did."

"He's probably waiting for the desperado to make another move and tip his hand," said Ed darkly. "Or maybe he is out looking, only we just haven't seen him. If he doesn't want us scared, he wouldn't be hanging around Camp Hancock."

"We'd have seen him, though," scoffed Mike. "Somebody would have."

"Not if you know the country. There are lots of places to hide if you know the country, and the sheriff does. I tell you it would be a cinch to keep out of sight. It would be easy for the desperado too. For all we know, he may be watching us day and night."

"What for?" laughed Mike. "So he can swipe your sleeping bag again?"

"You got desperadoes on the brain," accused Roger. "Who do you think you are, the Texas Ranger?"

"Sure he does," agreed Mike promptly. "Hi, Tex. Where's your gun, Tex?"

"Aw, dry up," said Ed feebly, wishing he had never mentioned his theory out loud.

But he had mentioned it, and it was something that the others refused to forget. Mike and Roger addressed him as Tex on every opportunity, and when the others asked the reason, the story spread fast. By the time they started back to camp everyone knew that Ed had said a desperado was still lurking around one of the rimrock ledges, and everyone was calling him Tex.

He gritted his teeth and tried to pretend he didn't care. Let them laugh. If the theory was true—but by this time he was beginning to doubt it himself—they'd laugh on the other side of their faces when trouble started. Meanwhile, he'd keep his idea about wild horses to himself. Even Duane would never know about that.

They stopped at the swimming hole for a quick swim, and it was practically dinnertime when the truck drove up in the open space under the flagpole. Those in the groups which had not gone to the mammal beds were waiting there, already cleaned up for the evening meal, and among them Ed recognized his cousin Priscilla.

Well, at least he had had one day without her tagging after him, he thought triumphantly. She must have changed her mind at the last minute, for he had seen her name on the sign-up list.

Ginny saw her, too, and began screaming at her immediately.

"Priscilla, come here. I've got something to tell you."

The passengers had to unload from the back of the truck, and since Ed had been one of the first to get on, he had to await his turn to get off. Priscilla had joined Ginny by that time, and they were standing close to the spot where he jumped to the ground.

"Priscilla, I want you to meet the Texas Ranger," cried Ginny, mischief shining in her eyes. "Do you know what he thinks? He actually thinks there's somebody hiding in the hills watching every move we make. Isn't he crazy?"

"Oh, you——" began Ed angrily, but he broke off suddenly, startled by something he saw in his cousin's face.

It wasn't fear exactly, nor was it disbelief, nor even the derision that he had seen all afternoon. It was closer to sympathy. She looks kind of tired, he thought in surprise, and not quite so prettied up, and almost human for a change.

"No," said Priscilla gently. "I don't think he's crazy. I don't think he's crazy at all."

Thirteen

"Don't skimp on those servings, girls," said Mrs. Hancock. "We want everyone to get enough to eat."

Priscilla obediently ladled a little more stew onto the plate. She might as well, for there was no way of carrying stew to Many Horse.

She had been pleased when she saw her name on the list for evening KP. Here was a real chance to secrete extra food for the Indian, who met her every night in the gully at the end of the swamp. So far the provisions she had taken him were only those things she could buy in the canteen or save from her own meals—candy bars, fruit, bread and butter, and cookies. Many Horse had accepted them, but he hadn't been hesitant about reminding her that they were a small return for the favor he had done her.

Because he was a savage and she had read that savages were children and couldn't understand such things, she didn't try to explain that the food she brought was the smallest part of the repayment. Because of him she had become a lawbreaker, a felon. Every night that she stole away alone, with a bread-and-butter sandwich and an apple in her pocket, she was breaking one of the major rules of camp. And the worst of it was that it was so easy. She had thought, when she crept back into camp unobserved after Many Horse had returned her to the swamp, that it was luck. Now she knew it wasn't luck at all. It was because the people around here were trusting. They were good people, with high standards, and they just couldn't believe that anyone would let them down. But Priscilla had let them down. She had broken the rules, and now it was a choice of continuing to do so or of breaking her promise to Many Horse. She hated herself, but she didn't know what to do about it.

If only the Indian wouldn't complain so about the food. Tonight she had hoped there would be roast. It would not have been too hard to set aside a couple of slices when no one was looking. Everyone knew that meat was the natural food of Indians, and she would have liked to please Many

Horse. He was really a very nice person and, when he wasn't grumbling about the short rations she provided, he was quite friendly.

He had told her many interesting things about his people, the Tyighs, who once owned all this part of the country. He had even confided that he was on a mission to prove his manhood, as the boys of his tribe had always done. He had left his father's tepee, and for two weeks he was supposed to live alone, off the bounty of the land.

Priscilla thought that candy bars and bread and butter from Camp Hancock could hardly be counted as bounty of the land, but she didn't suggest such a thing to Many Horse. After all, they must be just tidbits to supplement his regular diet. He had a bow and a quiver filled with arrows, which he told her he used to bring down birds and game. The arrows were tipped with points made of opal and obsidian, which he had carved himself last winter while he and the other young men sat about the lodge listening to the tales of the wise old men of the Tyighs.

"There. That's the last one," announced Ginny breathlessly, taking the filled plate from her. "You can dish up for us now. Everybody's served."

Priscilla nodded and began filling the plates which those who had helped with the dinner preparation held out for her. She filled her own last, then carried it to the end of the table where Ginny was saving her a place.

"Well, thank goodness we're through now," said Ginny, buttering a slice of bread. "We don't have to do dishes. I hate to wash dishes, even if it does get your hands good and clean."

Priscilla involuntarily glanced down at her own hands. The nails were no longer carefully filed, with the cuticle nicely pushed back. She knew they were clean, for she had washed them thoroughly before reporting for KP, but they were stained, and some of the nails were broken. Miss Barrett wouldn't have approved of her hands at all, but they didn't seem very important now.

"I wonder if the Texas Ranger did find a geode today," said Ginny. "Mr. Graves said it might possibly have something inside it, but the way Tex was carrying on it couldn't miss."

"I don't know," said Priscilla. "I hope so."

"You hope so?" Ginny put down her fork in surprise. "After the way he's treated you?"

"I feel a little sorry for him. Everybody's been ribbing him so. I don't think people ought to call him Tex the way they do. They ought to forget it."

"Well, if he hadn't kept insisting there was a bandit hanging around, they would," pointed out Ginny. "If there was somebody, we'd see him."

"Not necessarily," insisted Priscilla faintly. "It's

a big country, and it's easy enough to hide if you don't want to be seen."

"Fat chance," scoffed Ginny. She stopped speaking and watched quizzically as Priscilla made a sandwich of her bread and butter spread with jam, then folded the sandwich and her cupcake inside her paper napkin.

"That's the second time I've seen you do that. Are you afraid you'll starve before breakfast?"

"Sometimes I wake up during the night and I'm hungry," explained Priscilla uneasily. She wished she didn't have to lie to Ginny. Ginny was her friend, but she wouldn't be when she discovered what Priscilla really was. "It's part of my dinner. There's no law against taking it with me, is there?"

"I guess not," admitted Ginny.

There were to be movies that night as soon as it was dark enough for them to be seen on the outdoor screen. It would give her an opportunity to sneak away unobserved and deliver the food to Many Horse, but darkness was still a good hour from now.

"What'll we do?" demanded Ginny as they wandered out of the mess hall. "Let's walk down to the swamp and back."

"All right," agreed Priscilla reluctantly. Two trips to the swamp and back on top of the day's hike were quite a bit of walking, and she was already tired. Still, she couldn't say no to Ginny.

Then she jumped and squealed, as something darted out of nowhere and attached itself to her ankle.

"It's only Tufty," laughed Ginny, reaching down and detaching the furry gray ball which clung with tiny, needle-sharp claws to the tender skin above Priscilla's shoe tops.

"Well, I wish he wouldn't pick on me," admitted Priscilla ruefully.

Tufty was a wildcat kitten which had been given to Camp Hancock by two members of the Wildlife Service, who had visited there earlier in the week. He was gray-striped and fuzzy, with tiny tufts of hair on the end of each pointed ear, and small enough so that he could sit cupped in the palm of one's hand. Not that Tufty was content to sit in such a position. For all that he looked like an ordinary kitten, he refused to act like one. If he was picked up, he clawed to get down. If he was ignored, he immediately jumped on someone's lap, staring up with beautiful yellow eyes and purring with such a tremendous roar that it seemed impossible that such a sound could come from so small an animal.

He immediately struggled to be put down now, but Ginny clung fast.

"Let's feed him," she suggested. "Maybe he'll stay if we give him something to eat."

"There's probably stew left in the kitchen," agreed Priscilla.

Tufty was just a handful

"Why walk clear back there?" demanded Ginny. "Give him part of your sandwich. You'll never want it, and anyway, you have the cupcake too. It's in your pocket."

"No," objected Priscilla. "He doesn't like jam sandwiches. Cats are meat eaters."

"How do you know he doesn't like jam sandwiches? Did you ever try him on one?"

"No, but I know he doesn't like them," said Priscilla stiffly. "You know what those Wildlife men said. They said to feed him only cooked meat. If he gets raw meat, it will make him too wild."

"A jam sandwich isn't raw meat," pointed out Ginny. "Hurry up. He's clawing me."

"I don't want to," said Priscilla firmly.

Tufty won the argument by clawing himself free and jumping to the ground, where he darted out of sight under the mess-hall table. Ginny fingered the little V in the throat of her blouse where Tufty's struggles had left tiny red cuts.

"You're a pig," she said scornfully. "That's what you are, Priscilla Herrick. A stubborn pig!"

Priscilla watched her stalk away. She wanted to call her back and explain, but she couldn't. She couldn't tell even Ginny about Many Horse, who had to have the jam sandwich and the cupcake. Tufty got plenty to eat, and he probably wouldn't have liked it anyway. Now Ginny was angry with her, and Ginny was her best friend at camp. All the other girls were older, and they had their own best friends.

She didn't want to walk down to the edge of the swamp by herself, and Ginny had joined a large group under the flagpole. If Priscilla went there too, it would look as though she were tagging along. She hesitated a moment, then started toward the tent which was used as a workshop. It was usually filled at this time of day by those who were cleaning up their specimens from the morning's trip. Today had been unrewarding so far as Priscilla's own search was concerned. She hadn't found one new mineral to add to the collection in which she was beginning to take pride, but she could go to the workshop and inspect the discoveries of the others.

Tonight there were only three people inside the tent, and when she recognized them she would have turned back, but Mr. Graves looked up and saw her.

"Your cousin's found a geode," he called. "It's a nice one. Come and see."

"Tex hit pay dirt this time, all right," admitted Duane. "He's cutting it out now."

Ed looked up briefly before returning to his work. His mouth was stretched in a wide grin, which didn't even fade when he recognized her, and his eyes were shining with excitement.

"I knew it was one!" he cried happily. "I knew it."

Priscilla came inside cautiously and went over to stand beside Mr. Graves. Ed was working carefully. He sawed only a few strokes into the rock, then stopped to inspect what he had done.

"The crystal seems to be in the form of a little dish," explained Mr. Graves. "That's why he had to be so careful getting it out."

"See!" exclaimed Ed proudly. He took the rock from under the saw and thrust it toward her. "Isn't it a beauty?"

Remembering how he had resented her handling the specimens in his own workroom, she refrained from touching it, leaning over to inspect it in his hands.

"Why, it is," she cried in surprise. "It's going to be lovely when you get it sawed out."

"Take it," invited Ed cordially. "You can't see down into it unless you hold it."

She took the half-opened rock respectfully in her hands and stared into its shimmering heart.

"It's quartz! Oh, I hope you don't break it getting it out."

"That's why he's going so slow," Duane told her. "He'll be all night the way he's going. And we'll miss the movies."

"Who cares about the movies?" scoffed Ed. "Not when they've got a geode like this."

"I do," said Duane flatly. He winked at Priscilla to let her know that geodes weren't so terribly important. "And I'm going to this one. 'By, Priscilla, Mr. Graves. See you later, Tex."

Priscilla saw Ed scowl a little as she returned the geode, but she knew it wasn't meant for her. No one would enjoy being called Tex, not when it was a rib. Besides, she thought, while Ed wasn't entirely right, he wasn't entirely wrong either. The camp was being observed, only by an Indian, not a bandit.

"I'm going to have to run along too, Ed," said Mr. Graves. "There are several things I have to attend to tonight. You can keep on the way you're going. Just be careful."

Watching him go, Priscilla wondered if she should leave too, but she didn't quite know where to go. She didn't want to return to the group Ginny was with, at least not while Ginny was angry. It was still too light to take the food to Many Horse. Probably Ed wished she would go away, but he hadn't said so. Maybe he didn't even remember she was still here.

She regarded him furtively, thinking that somehow he had changed since they had been at camp. He didn't seem quite so grubby and dirty or maybe it was because everybody else up here looked that way too. You couldn't get really clean in cold water, and who wanted to take the time to heat it on the stove?

"There!" said Ed suddenly. "I've got that side off. Look, isn't it a beauty?"

He had cut off the top and one side of the surrounding gray rock, and now it was easy to see the form of the crystal within. It was, as Mr. Graves had said, shaped like a small dish, curved ever so slightly at the sides and flat on the very bottom.

"Oh, it is," cried Priscilla in admiration. "Oh, Ed, you're so lucky. It looks like something in a jeweler's window."

"I know," he said humbly. "It's what I wanted more than anything, but I really didn't expect to find one. At least not one as nice as this."

"Not many people do find one as nice as this. I'll never have one in my collection."

The minute she said it she wished she could recall the words. She hadn't meant to let him know she had started a collection. He would think she was copying. To her surprise, he didn't seem to.

"What have you got so far?" he inquired casually.

"Not much," she admitted. "Some quartz and calcite and agate. And a piece of petrified wood. That's my best piece."

"No opal?"

She shook her head.

"Here," he said, fumbling in his pocket. "I found a fair piece of opal today, before I found the geode. You might as well have it."

"Oh, but, Ed, I don't want to take your specimen."

"Take it, take it!" He dismissed the gift with an embarrassed wave of his hand, returning once more to his work. "I've got plenty of opal. You'll find some yourself before we go, probably. It's not too scarce."

"Well, thanks," she said, a little embarrassed herself. "If you're sure you don't want it, I might as well polish it up now. So long as I'm here, anyway."

Fourteen

The movie was well under way by the time Priscilla remembered that Many Horse would be waiting. Beyond an occasional comment on the progress of their work, she and Ed had not exchanged much conversation, but just the same it had been a pleasant and rather surprising interlude. He wasn't nearly so bad as she had imagined. He hadn't been rude to her once. She had expected at least a few caustic comments when he learned that she, too, was collecting rocks and minerals, but he seemed to take it for granted. And it was certainly nice of him to give her the piece of opal. It was a good specimen and was polishing up very well indeed.

She came out of the tent and stopped to observe the large group sitting on the ground under the flagpole. They were watching the movies on the screen which had been set up a little distance away, but the viewing would not be at its best, for an almost full moon had risen in the east, bathing the whole country in its soft, clear light.

In a way Priscilla was glad of the moon, for it was scary walking in pitch-darkness to the edge of the swamp, then cutting around to the gully behind. On the other hand, in all this moonlight she would be plainly visible for some distance, since there was nothing to provide cover except an occasional clump of sage. She would just have to hope that the movie was interesting enough to hold everyone's attention and that it would last long enough for her to go and return.

She started out, half expecting to hear someone call her name, but no one did. This was how it was with criminals, she told herself. They broke one law, then to cover up that mistake they had to keep on breaking more and more. Each time it grew a little more serious. She had heard that it grew a little easier each time a criminal broke a law, but it wasn't working that way for her. It was still hard on her conscience.

By the time she reached the barbwire fence which marked the beginnings of the swamp, she knew that she was safe. Camp Hancock was three quarters of a mile behind her, and while the moonlight was revealing, she certainly couldn't be seen at this distance.

The swamp looked eerie and foreboding tonight. In the daytime its reeds and rushes were richly green against the surrounding parched and arid land. It always made her feel cooler and more refreshed just to see them growing there. Now the moonlight drained them of color, and they thrust their stiff spires against a silver sky like an army of threatening spears. The ever-present frog chorus, which had made her laugh the first time she and Ginny had walked as far as the fence, was ominous too. They seemed to be croaking, "Shame, shame, shame."

She tried to close her ears and started walking along the fence. If only she could have crossed the swamp directly, she would have saved herself a quarter-mile walk; but the swamp was out of bounds, and she had broken enough rules as it was. It salved her conscience a little to obey this one.

At this point the rushes thinned out a little, and she had a glimpse through them to the very spot where she must deliver the food. There was a flash of something white, and she hurried on with a sense of relief. The white splotch was part of Lightning Bolt's coat, and she no longer felt quite so alone.

Many Horse was glad to see her, but he was also a little annoyed.

"Squaw late," he accused.

"I know," she admitted, fumbling in her pocket

for the napkin-wrapped parcel of food. "I was polishing some opal, and I forgot about the time."

Both the sandwich and the cupcake were smashed flat, but Many Horse did not comment on that at the moment. He unwrapped them swiftly and gobbled them down as fast as he could. He acted as though he were actually starving, Priscilla thought. Perhaps his hunting that day had not been too successful. As soon as he finished, he demanded more.

"I don't have anything else," she explained. "That's all I could bring. I'm out of spending money, so I can't buy anything from the canteen. I've already spent all I had on you."

"You gotta bring more than this," he insisted.

"There wasn't anything else I could bring," she said patiently. "After all, our bargain was for me to bring you *some* food every night. We didn't say how much."

"Huh," he grunted. "Squaw bring more. Lots more."

"But I can't. I have to bring you part of my own dinner. Tonight we had stew. I couldn't carry that, could I?"

"Bring pan," he suggested. Then he added a little accusingly, "Sandwich all squashed."

"I have to carry things in my pocket. They'd see me carrying a pan out of camp," she told him. "I'm not supposed to be leaving camp at all. I'm breaking a rule to come here anyway."

"Squaw promise," he reminded her quickly.

"I know. And I'll keep my promise. Maybe tomorrow night they'll have roast and I can bring you some of that."

He nodded grudgingly, and she got to her feet. It would never do to stay too long. At all costs, she must get back before it was time for the campers to go to their tents for the night.

"Squaw not go now," scowled Many Horse. "Stay awhile. Me tell you about my people."

"I can't stay tonight, Many Horse. I was late getting here, and I have to hurry back before I'm missed. See, I was polishing this piece of opal. It's like the way you used to make some of your arrowheads."

She found the half-polished specimen in her pocket and held it out for him to see. Many Horse took it from her, turning it over in his hand.

"Squaw make arrowhead?" he demanded, returning it to her at last.

"Oh no," she laughed. "I'm not clever like you. Besides, I have no need for arrowheads. I just like it the way it is. I collect rocks and minerals."

He seemed to be thinking this over for a moment. Then he motioned to her to wait and walked over to where Lightning Bolt was standing.

"Squaw took gift. Can't give back. Bad luck to break potlatch."

She saw him fumbling in the saddlebag, then he returned and held out a rough, dark object.

"Many Horse give present to squaw," he announced. "This obsidian. My people use for arrowheads. This piece no good for that. Won't chip. You take."

Priscilla took the black stone from his hand. It felt like hard, smooth glass. It was about three inches at the longest place and perhaps two inches across and had obviously been broken from a larger piece. She had never seen any obsidian, but she remembered reading about it in the books which Mr. Graves had lent her. At the moment she couldn't remember exactly what it was she had read.

"Thank you, Many Horse," she said. "I do appreciate this."

"Then Squaw bring Many Horse much food tomorrow," he said quickly. "Potlatch Indian custom. You get gift, you give bigger gift. Squaw bring Many Horse much food."

"Oh dear!" She felt trapped and tried to give the obsidian back to him. "Then I'd better not take it, because I don't know how much I can bring. I'll bring what I can, but you don't expect me to steal it, do you?"

"Squaw took gift. Can't give back," he said triumphantly. He put his hands behind him and stepped back. "Bad luck to break potlatch. Very bad. You bring bigger gift next time."

"All right," she sighed, jamming the obsidian into her pocket with the opal and turning to go. "I'll do the very best I can."

"Come early," Many Horse shouted after her. "Come as soon as you can. And bring lots to eat."

Fifteen

"You found anything good yet?" called Duane.

Ed put down his hammer and clenched and unclenched his fingers, which were beginning to feel cramped.

"Nothing new. I just dug out a piece of something that looks like golden calcite, but I've already got some of that."

"Trouble with you, Tex, is you can't keep your mind on your work," yelled one of the campers, who was working nearby. "You have to keep one eye open for bandits."

Ed gritted his teeth and went back to work, ignoring the remark. These guys around here ran a joke into the ground. They went on and on about something they thought was funny, when it wasn't really funny at all. He had been careful to say no more about the dangerous fugitives spying on the camp, but the others kept bringing it up. Most of them seemed to have forgotten his real name, for everyone called him Tex. Even Duane called him that, and occasionally Mr. Graves forgot and addressed him that way. Only his cousin Priscilla remembered to say "Ed."

It was funny about Priscilla. She had certainly changed since she came out here. She wasn't the same person at all. Last night in the workshop, when she had been admiring his geode, he almost forgot she was a girl. She had worked away at the polishing wheel as matter-of-factly as Duane might have done.

Ed was glad he had given her the opal. It was a good piece and, outside of the petrified wood, probably the best in her collection. Maybe he'd give her the golden calcite he had just found. There was no harm in helping the kid along a little, so long as she was trying to be a good guy.

At noon he made up his mind that he might as well make the presentation right then. Somebody had started up the rib again, pretending he saw a figure skulking along the top of a distant rimrock. It was easier to walk off than argue, so he got to his feet and wandered down the cliff toward the spot where the girls were eating their lunch.

To his surprise, Priscilla wasn't with Ginny today. She was sitting by herself, her back propped against the ledge where she had been working, her legs in their dirty blue jeans straight out in front of her. At first he pretended not to see her. He walked along as though he were inspecting the cliff, possibly with an eye to changing his site of operation. Then he allowed his eyes to fall accidentally upon her sitting there. He pretended to look surprised, and stopped directly in front of her.

"Hi," he said in a noncommittal tone. "Have any luck?"

"Not compared to what you found yesterday," she told him shyly. "Did you finish cutting out your geode after I left?"

"Yeah. It turned out pretty well," he admitted, attempting to sound offhand about it. "Of course you can't expect to find a geode here, if that's what you're looking for."

"I know it. I'm just looking for calcite," she agreed meekly.

"I found a piece of the golden this morning. I've got plenty of it already, so if you want it you can have it," he said. His voice came out gruffly because he was embarrassed, but Priscilla didn't seem to notice.

"I'd love to have it," she said quickly. "But you already gave me the opal last night, and it's not fair for me to keep taking your specimens. I ought to trade for them at least. That's what the others do."

"Oh, that's okay." He waved off her protests, tossed the calcite-laden rock in her direction, and turned to go.

"Wait," she called quickly. "I mean it. About trading."

"What have you got to trade? You don't mean your petrified wood."

"Oh no," she cried in alarm. "I just couldn't trade that. But—do you have any obsidian?"

"No."

"Then here, you take this," she said quickly. "I can always get more like it."

It took her a moment to extract the jagged black stone from her pocket, for its rough edges had caught on the material. Then she held it out to him triumphantly. He turned it over and over in his hand, looking a little puzzled.

"Where'd you get this?" he demanded curiously. "Not here? Not today?"

"Oh no. Not here," she said quickly. "I found it before. I'm not sure now where it did come from. I didn't mark it when I got back to camp, you see."

"Then you can't get more of it."

"Oh, I'm sure I can," she smiled.

"Then you'll have to remember where you found it," he insisted. "So far as anybody knows there's no obsidian around here. It's only found in lava formations. From igneous rock."

She stared at him helplessly. All too late she

remembered what the books said about obsidian. How could she have been so stupid as to claim she had found it around these sedimentary cliffs? Even the basalt in the Clarno Basin yielded no obsidian.

"I'd better go show Mr. Graves," cried Ed in excitement. "You're sure you want to trade? You don't have to, you know."

"I'm sure," agreed Priscilla miserably.

Mr. Graves was interested in the obsidian, but he agreed with Ed that it hadn't come from the Clarno Basin.

"It was probably carried in years ago by the Indians," he decided. "We sometimes find chips and arrowheads around here made of obsidian, but these Indians went a long way to get it. They usually used opal to tip their arrows. Probably this was just one piece that dropped from some warrior's pack as he was on his way home. It's kicked around all these years, and Priscilla uncovered it."

"That was pretty smart of her," admitted Ed. Then he grinned widely. "Anyway, it's mine now. It was her idea to trade."

As the afternoon wore on, however, he began to wonder about it. Priscilla had said she could get more obsidian. She had spoken as though she were quite sure of herself. How could she get more if this was just one fragment dropped long ago by some ancient arrowhead maker?

He took the specimen she had given him from

the sack where he kept his rocks and inspected it once more, hoping to find a clue there. On one side there was a series of small cuts and scratches, as though someone had tried unsuccessfully to chip the obsidian with a knife. That, at least, substantiated Mr. Grave's theory, but Ed didn't feel that it was enough. Perhaps Priscilla's hammer had made those marks when she broke this fragment from a larger piece. Perhaps she had found a whole ledge of obsidian somewhere, and she was keeping it a secret from the others. He couldn't imagine why she would do such a thing, but maybe it was because she was a girl; girls thought differently from boys. It was too bad to discover this streak of selfishness in his cousin just as he was beginning to like her a little, but there it was. Such a find should be public knowledge, and since Priscilla apparently didn't intend to tell anyone, it was up to him.

But where could she have found the deposit? What opportunity had she had? He tried to think back over the past twelve days. She had been a member of every field trip he himself had been on, except one. She hadn't gone to the mammal beds. That must have been when she made the discovery. He would have to find out where she went that day before he could narrow down the search.

He could have talked with her during the hike back to camp, for he saw that she and Ginny were not walking together as they usually did. It would be a simple matter to catch up with Priscilla, but he would feel silly walking with a girl, so he stayed with Duane. And when they reached camp, the matter was erased temporarily from his mind, for the sheriff was waiting for them.

Ed's hopes soared when he recognized the wind-roughened face under the broad-brimmed hat. Perhaps the sheriff had come to admit that his theory of a tramp had been wrong. Perhaps he was ready at last to make public the news of a capture.

"I'd like to ask your help," said the sheriff, speaking to Mr. Hancock but keeping his voice high so they could all hear. "There may be a lost boy wandering around in these parts. While you're out prospecting, I'd like you to keep your eyes open."

"It's easy enough to get lost around here," said Mr. Hancock gravely. "What about this boy?"

"His name's Johnny Chapin. He's about twelve, and he's probably not around here at all," admitted the sheriff. "He's from over at Wamic, which is fifty or seventy-five miles from here, too far for a boy to walk. His horse was in the corral, so he must be afoot. They've gone all over that part of the country without any luck, and now they're widening the search."

"Poor boy," said Mr. Hancock sympathetically. "Any of you campers seen a strange boy wandering around here?"

"Maybe he was the one who swiped my——" began Ed. He fell silent as the other campers began exchanging knowing smiles. Let them laugh, he decided. After all, it did seem rather unlikely now that he thought of it.

"I want you all to think about this boy's experience in terms of yourselves," said Mr. Hancock gravely when the sheriff had gone. "Here's a boy who knows this type of country thoroughly. He's probably lived here all his life. If he can get lost, just think what might happen to you. That's why we made the rule about never going out alone."

Ed's glance happened to fall on his cousin at this moment, and he had never seen anyone look so uncomfortable. Guilt was written on every line of her flushed face. She had been up to something all right, he told himself. It must be even worse than he thought, but it explained the obsidian. She'd been off on her own when she found it, so now she was afraid to admit the discovery. He'd just have to get her alone and see what he could pump out of her.

Priscilla herself finally gave him an opportunity to talk with her at the swimming hole. He had grown tired of swimming and gone to sit on the bank to catch his breath, when she walked out of the river. Much to his surprise, she headed straight for him.

"Hi," she said shyly. "The water feels good today, doesn't it?"

"Yeah," he agreed. Then he added, a little stiffly, "Sit down if you want to."

She sat down on the bank beside him, and Ed looked about him hastily. No one seemed to be paying any attention to the fact that he was sitting with a girl. Anyway, she was his cousin, so he guessed it was all right to sit beside her and talk for a while.

"Camp's about over," she said. "Just one more day, and we'll go home. I had a card from Aunt Margaret. She'll be there by the time we are."

"I got one too," he agreed absently. How in the heck could he go about finding out where she was the day he went to the mammal beds? If he just came right out and asked, she might get suspicious.

"You know, I was wrong about this camp," Priscilla admitted. "I didn't really want to come, and I didn't like rocks either. But I do now. I think they're very interesting."

"Did you get all the specimens you wanted?" he asked slyly. "You've only got one more day to gather up any that you're missing."

"I know," she sighed.

"You didn't go with us when we took the truck to the old mammal beds, did you?" he asked boldly.

"No. No, I didn't."

"Where did you go that day?" he demanded.

Since he hadn't been able to think of another way, there was nothing else to do but come right out and ask.

"I wanted to go to the agate beds," she said evasively, and her tone added to his suspicions.

"Is that where you went?"

"No," she admitted after a moment. "I was late getting started. The others went on without me. I didn't get to look for specimens that day." She

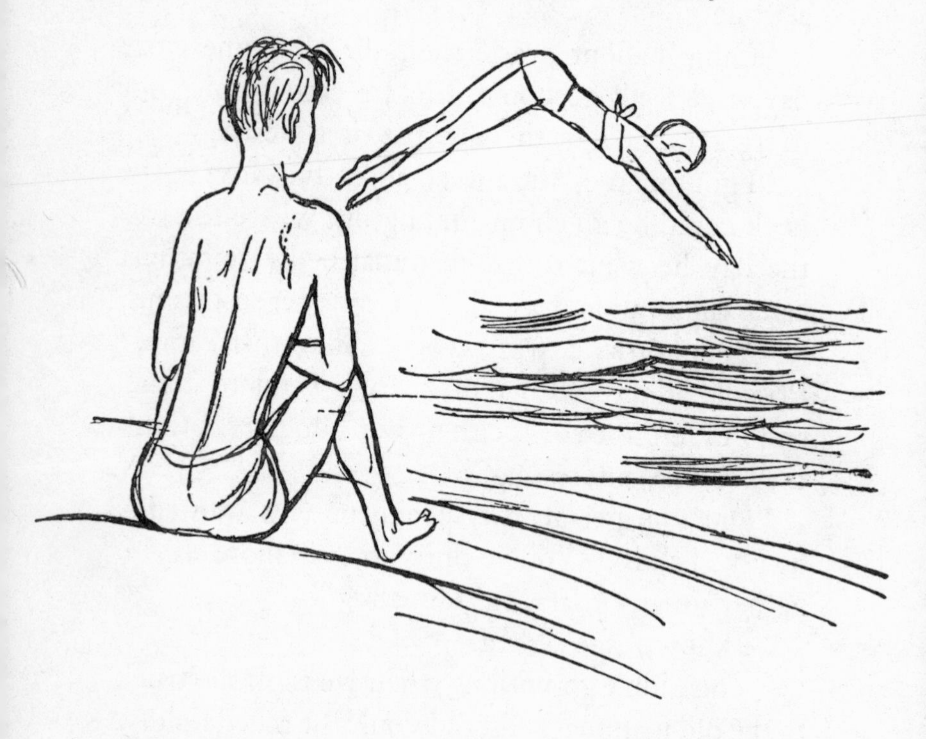

Ed watched her perfect dive into the river with reluctant admiration

got to her feet, ending the discussion. "They'll be going back to camp soon. I'm going in the water again."

Ed watched her perfect dive into the river with reluctant admiration. She was a really good swimmer. He wished he were half as good, but at least he was honest and aboveboard. Priscilla wasn't. She must have disobeyed the rules and gone off on her own that day. Since she hadn't got lost, a very easy thing to do, as witness that boy the sheriff was looking for, she must have stayed fairly close to camp. The deposit of obsidian must be right under their noses, and Priscilla would undoubtedly return to get another specimen for herself.

His course was clear now. All he had to do was keep her under constant surveillance until he found out for himself.

Sixteen

Private eyes didn't have it as easy as Ed had imagined. He admitted as much to himself as he settled down on the fringe of campers collected about the bonfire. Priscilla finally had sat down, and he had begun to think she never would. Of course he really didn't have to start his sleuthing until tomorrow morning, but it was just as well to get in a little preliminary practice tonight. She certainly wouldn't try to sneak away from camp at this hour. Dusk was beginning to gather, and despite the light of a full moon, no one in his right mind, especially a timid girl, would take off after dark.

So far Priscilla had led him a busy chase. After dinner she had gone to the kitchen end of the mess hall, where she had talked sometime with Mrs. Hancock. Then she had gone to her own tent and emerged later wearing an old white jacket which had once belonged to Ed. He recognized it immediately, and with some regret, for he had been sorry when it grew too tight for him through the shoulders. He'd never had another jacket he liked as well, nor one with such commodious pockets. After that Priscilla went to the workshop, and Ed had been able to follow her there openly. All the wheels and saws had been occupied, which meant she couldn't work on the golden calcite, so she had gone back outside.

No movies were scheduled for tonight, and the bonfire was kindled early, even before it was quite dark. Not until then did Priscilla sit down, and Ed had the feeling that she was only perching temporarily, as though at any moment she might get up and start roaming around once more.

The dry juniper crackled and the flames, dissolving the first gray puffs of smoke, shot upward. They looked pretty against the rapidly graying sky; and perhaps the other campers thought so too, for a sudden stillness fell on the group. Somewhere, way off in the desert, a coyote howled, and then there was another sound, much closer, which made everyone jump. It was a little like a whoop and a threatening howl all in one. Then a bent figure dressed in rags, with wild flying hair, darted from one of the tents. Those who were attending their first session screamed and fell back in alarm, but the experienced campers grinned at each other. It was Mr. Hancock giving a history lesson, one that would stay in their minds much longer than the printed pages of a book.

Once a year he dressed up in this way and told them the story of John Day, the Kentucky frontiersman for whom this valley and its largest river had been named. No boy or girl would ever forget, after hearing Mr. Hancock's story, about John Jacob Astor's attempt to plant an American colony in Oregon Territory. They would always remember that while the expedition by sea arrived safely at the spot now called Astoria, the second group, which tried to come overland, was not so successful. The members of this party had died, one after another, from starvation and by Indian tomahawks; and the only two survivors, one of whom was John Day, were finally rescued by the sea party in this very valley, where they had managed to survive the winter.

Ed was glad that Priscilla was going to hear the story. It would be something for her to remember when she got back home. He looked over to see if she had recovered from her fright of the ragged apparition, and had to shake himself. Priscilla was gone.

At first he thought she might be hiding behind

someone else, still quaking with fear, but there was no place for her to hide. Everyone had recovered and was laughing heartily, squeezing together to make room for Mr. Hancock at the fire. They were all so occupied with him that they didn't think to look beyond their own circle, but Ed looked. He saw Priscilla's small figure, quite obvious in the white jacket, striking out toward the swamp and fast disappearing in the twilight.

He got to his feet, hesitating as he stared after her. That stupid girl! What did she think she was doing, anyway? This was no time to go after obsidian, or anything else. He knew that he ought to sound an alarm, to tell the others that Priscilla had ignored camp rules and started out alone after dark, but he couldn't quite bring himself to do so. He didn't know what punishment would be exacted, probably something very dire indeed. Small infractions were punished by KP duty, but campers just didn't break big rules.

Still, Priscilla was different. She deliberately stretched them to the breaking point. He remembered the day she had strained the rule by diving off the bridge into the very boundary of the pool. That was bad enough, but this was even worse. She must be brought back immediately.

He opened his mouth to say something, looking around vaguely for someone in authority. Mr. Hancock had already started his story. It was new to this year's instructors, and they seemed to be listening eagerly. So were the campers, even those who had heard it before.

Perhaps it would be better to bring her back himself, he decided. He could do it quietly, administering at the same time a good, strong lecture on the subject, and no one would have to know. After all, Priscilla was his cousin and, as his mother had intimated more than once, his responsibility.

He started out after her. No one saw him go, so no one called after him. If they had just done that, he would have explained. Since they didn't, it was a little their fault too. They ought to pay more attention to what was going on.

Priscilla was completely out of sight by this time, hidden by the twilight. She must have been running, he decided, to get this far ahead, but she had been going toward the swamp all right. The obsidian deposit must be behind that, perhaps in the rimrock pinnacles they called the Palisades, since there was nothing else to yield minerals between here and there. It was hard to believe that she was going as far as the Palisades, but if she was he must overtake her before she got there. Although the moonlight was revealing, it was also deceptive, and it would be easy enough for her to conceal herself against the rocks.

He ran on, hoping to overtake her, but somehow she kept her distance. He resented people, like

Duane and Priscilla, whose legs had grown longer than his. Never mind. One of these days he'd start growing, and then he'd pass them both up. He'd really show them then.

He knew that he was approaching the swamp, even before he arrived, by the sound of the frogs. They were particularly noisy tonight, as though they had been disturbed by something. Maybe it was Priscilla who had disturbed them, he thought grimly. Maybe she had actually gone into the swamp itself. Apparently she was crazy enough to do anything.

When he came to the fence, he stopped, trying to decide which way she had gone. It must have been to the right, for if she had turned left she would still be in sight, since the swamp extended farther in that direction. He blamed himself for the long period of hesitation by the bonfire while he made up his mind what to do. If he'd only started the moment he saw her, he would surely have overtaken her by this time.

He turned right and hurried on, panting from his long run and keeping his eyes open. Then he stopped short, for at a place where the rushes thinned and grew less thickly he caught a glimpse of something white on the other side. It was visible for only a moment before it was gone, but he knew what it was. It was his own white jacket! Priscilla had completed the curve of the swamp. She had come out on the other side, and now she was heading straight for the Palisades.

He would never catch her now. Not unless—— But he couldn't do that. He couldn't cut across the corner of the swamp. It was a bog, and dangerous. It was filled with springs, and rattlesnakes came there to drink. Besides, it was forbidden, out of bounds.

Desperately he peered through the rushes. There weren't very many of them here. They didn't grow so thickly, which meant that the ground must be drier. The snakes would be closer to the springs, not here where there was nothing to drink.

He lifted the single strand of barbwire and crawled between it and the fence.

The ground was quite dry for several paces, then it began to stick to his feet. Still, it wasn't too bad. It was no worse than the vacant lot where they played ball after a heavy rain. Nettles reached out and caught at his jeans, trying to hold him back, but he pulled away and went on, even ignoring one which fastened its stinging barbs on his bare ankle. There would be time to take care of that when he caught up with Priscilla.

He was well into the swamp now, and the rushes grew more thickly than they had appeared from the fence. He had to push them aside to get through, and with each step his shoes sank deeper into the wet mud. It made a curious sucking sound each time he lifted his dripping tennis shoes and set them down again; and then, without warning, he discovered that he couldn't lift them any more. They were stuck fast in the mud, and he was sinking even deeper.

He tried to pull himself loose by grabbing hold of the rushes, but they only broke off in his fingers.

The mud came up to his knees by now

The mud was up to his knees by now. If he stood perfectly still and didn't struggle, he didn't seem to sink any deeper, but that was too much to ask of anyone. He couldn't just stand here, knee-deep in mud until morning. Besides, what if he should fall down? The mud would cover him completely, and no one would ever know what had happened to him.

There was nothing to do but call for help, and he did. He opened his mouth and yelled as loudly as he could, hoping that Priscilla, on her way to the Palisades, would hear him.

"Help! Help!" he yelled. "Priscilla, help! It's me. Ed. I'm stuck in the swamp. Help!"

Seventeen

When she heard there would be no movies this evening, Priscilla had been afraid she would have no opportunity of slipping away from camp, but things had been easier than she imagined. It was probably due to the coolness which still existed between her and Ginny, for no one paid much attention to her now. The others were friendly enough, but no one sought her out as Ginny had done. She could be with them or not, and it didn't seem to matter. Now Ginny didn't care either, and it made her feel like a lonesome outsider. Even the guarded truce which she and Ed were observing didn't make up for the loss of her best friend in camp. She was glad that they would be here only one more day.

At least Many Horse would be glad to see her

this evening, and she would be able to repay the gift of obsidian. Perhaps he might even be persuaded to give her an extra piece. There had been roast for dinner, and not only had she saved her own serving, together with a bread-and-butter sandwich, but Mrs. Hancock had cut an extra slice for her after dinner. Priscilla had told Mrs. Hancock she was still hungry, which was certainly the truth, since she had skimped so on dinner, so everything was open and aboveboard too. Then she remembered how Many Horse had complained about the sandwich and cupcake being mashed from carrying them in her jeans, so she had gone to her tent for the white jacket with the big pockets.

She would have liked to start out early, but she didn't dare. An after-dinner hike to the edge of the swamp and back was a favorite pastime with too many of the campers. She couldn't walk there alone, nor could she go with anyone else and not return in their company. She just had to wait until everyone had returned and was occupied with something else.

The campers were especially gay tonight. Perhaps they realized that this was almost their last evening, and they were determined to make the most of it. There had never been quite so many jokes going around nor so much hilarity as there was tonight. Priscilla could have joined in, but since she didn't the others left her alone.

When the light was applied to the paper under the kindling and the juniper boughs began to creak in protest, she rose quietly and walked away. It was as simple as that.

There was one moment of panic when she thought she had been discovered, for she heard an ear-splitting screech behind her. She whirled around, expecting to be called back, but at that moment there was a roar of laughter from those around the campfire, so she knew the cry had not been for her. Nevertheless, she ought to get to the gully and back as quickly as possible, so she began to run.

She reached the fence and began circling the end of the swamp. How beautiful everything was, bathed in moonlight. Against a translucent sky, the rimrock pinnacles of the Palisades loomed large and dark above the swamp, like a rough drawing made in charcoal. The hard, rutty ground over which she had just come seemed to have smoothed itself out as she looked back. It lay like a carpet of dull silver which was finally swallowed up in a night that had one tiny red eye, the bonfire back at Camp Hancock.

She had almost reached the gully where Many Horse would be waiting, when she thought she heard someone calling her name. Involuntarily she slowed down and turned half around. It was probably those dreadful frogs, she thought. Then she heard it again.

"Priscilla! Help!"

That couldn't be the frogs, although the cry had certainly come from the swamp behind her. She listened, and the voice came again, the words carrying clearly on the desert air.

"Help! Help! It's me, Ed. I'm stuck in the swamp. Help!"

"Who's that?" demanded a new voice, and she realized that Many Horse also had heard the cry. He had left the gully and raced out to meet her.

"It's my cousin," she said quickly. "At least he says that's who it is."

"Did you bring him here?" frowned Many Horse. "Did you tell him about me?"

"No, no," she protested quickly. "I didn't tell a soul. He must have followed me."

"Help!" called the voice from the swamp. "Help! I'm sinking."

"I've got to go see," she told Many Horse quickly. "I'll be back."

But Many Horse came with her. Together they raced to the fence surrounding the swamp and, straining their eyes, tried to see inside. The rushes obscured their view, and they could see nothing at all.

"Ed!" cried Priscilla. "Is that you? What are you doing?"

"I'm stuck in the mud," came his frantic voice. "It's up to my knees. I can't lift either foot to get out."

"But what were you doing going past the fence, anyway?" she called helplessly. "You know we're not allowed in the swamp."

"Following you," he howled. "It's all your fault. I followed you and thought this would be a short cut. Go get help before I sink in over my head. Hurry up."

"Yes, yes," she shouted. "I'll go. I'll go right now. You wait right there."

"Never mind," said Many Horse. He spoke crossly, but there was a note of resignation, too, in his voice. "I'll get him out of there. Wait till I get Lightning Bolt."

"Who was that?" called Ed instantly. "Who were you talking to?"

"It's a friend of mine," shrieked Priscilla. "An Indian named Many Horse. He's going to help us. He's got a rope on his saddle, and his horse isn't far away. He'll pull you out."

"An Indian!" shouted Ed in amazement. "Where'd you meet an Indian?"

"Here. A few days ago. He's on a quest to prove his manhood. It's a custom of his tribe. He's been living around here, off the country, for a couple of weeks. I've been bringing him extra things to eat. That's where I was going tonight."

"You mean he's been hanging around here and none of us saw him? Nobody but you?"

"That's all. Only you suspected him, Ed. You suspected all the time that somebody was watching the camp, and there was."

"Well, what do you know!" Even at this distance she could detect the pleased satisfaction in his voice.

Many Horse returned in a few moments leading Lightning Bolt. He had the coil of rope, which customarily hung on the saddle, in his hands.

"Have you located him yet?" he demanded. "Where is he?"

"His voice comes from that clump of reeds. I can't see him, though."

Many Horse nodded. He tied one end of the rope to the saddle horn, then, keeping the coil in his hands, crawled gingerly through the strands of the fence.

"Where are you, tenderfoot?" he shouted. His voice sounded very scornful.

"Right here," answered Ed meekly. "Don't come too close. You'll get stuck too."

"I know what I'm doing, even if you don't," snapped Many Horse. He advanced cautiously over the soggy ground, testing the mud before he took each new step.

"Can you see him?" called Priscilla anxiously. "Oh, be careful."

Many Horse advanced a few cautious steps more before he answered.

"I can't go any farther," he told them both. "But this is far enough. I can get a rope over him from here. Just stand still now."

Priscilla held her breath. The reeds moved back and forth, and she knew that Many Horse was doing something with the coil of rope. Then she saw his arm raise. Above the rushes and reeds, the loop spun up and out, a thin dark line barely visible in the moonlight. A moment later she heard Ed's surprised grunt.

"How's that?" called Many Horse.

"It's around me," Ed told him in a surprised voice. "Why don't you pull me out?"

"Hold still," said Many Horse impatiently. "Lightning Bolt will do that. He used to be a cow pony when he was younger. You're going to get kind of wet, so don't be surprised. You're facing that way, and we're pulling from this direction. But we can't be too particular about how we haul you out."

"Okay," agreed Ed. "I don't care how you do it so long as I get out of here."

Many Horse waded back across the damp ground and once more climbed through the fence.

"Come on, Lightning Bolt," he said.

As the black and white pony fell back, the rope began to straighten out. Priscilla watched it, so fascinated she hardly breathed. From the direction of the reeds there was a plopping squash and a muffled cry from Ed. The taut rope had jerked at that moment, but now it moved steadily on.

"Let me up! Let me up!" screamed Ed. "It's firm ground here. I won't sink now. Let me up."

"Stop, Many Horse!" Priscilla turned to relay

"We can't be too particular about how we haul you out of the swamp."

the message, and the Indian waved that he understood. She could see his teeth showing white in the moonlight. Many Horse was obviously enjoying himself thoroughly.

A few moments later Ed stalked from the swamp, dripping brown mud at every step. The first pull had thrown him on his back, and the mud had splashed up and almost covered him completely. In the moonlight he looked as though he had been dipped in a bath of soft chocolate.

Recoiling his rope, Many Horse returned to the fence. He looked at Ed and burst out laughing.

"This is my cousin Ed," introduced Priscilla quickly. "It's lucky you were here, Many Horse. You saved his life."

"Is he the one?" sputtered Ed, trying to wipe some of the mud from his face. "I thought you said there was an Indian here."

"Of course. Many Horse is an Indian. He belongs to the Tyigh tribe."

"He doesn't look like any Indian I ever saw—or even sound like one," objected Ed. "I bet he's the lost boy the sheriff's looking for."

"I am not lost. I've known where I was all the time," said Many Horse indignantly. "And if I don't look like a full-blooded Indian, it's not my fault. My great-great-great-grandmother was a full-blooded Tyigh. Her father was a chief named Many Horse. He ruled all the Tyigh valley and clear over here into the Clarno Basin. If he hadn't let his daughter marry a white man, and they hadn't kept on marrying white men, I'd have been a full blood all right."

"Don't get sore," said Ed hastily. "After all, Priscilla says you've been living like an Indian, eating off the land and all that. So if you want to be one it's okay with me."

"I'm not sure that I do," admitted the other boy after a moment. "Things were probably different around here in Many Horse's time. The first few days were okay because I had some food with me, and I could get supplies from your camp and leave money to pay. Then I ran out of money, and it wouldn't have been right to take things without paying. She"—nodding toward Priscilla—"doesn't bring me enough to feed a canary. I think I'll just go back home. I'd sure like to have a steak. And some mashed potatoes and gravy. And some pie."

"Why don't you go back to camp with us now?" suggested Ed. "Mrs. Hancock would see that you got something to eat tonight."

Priscilla looked from one to another in amazement. The conversation had been so fast, so unexpected, that she had trouble following, although both boys seemed to understand each other perfectly.

"But your quest," she stammered. "Are you going to give up your quest, Many Horse? Just like that?"

He looked at her thoughtfully, then his face brightened.

"I think I'll go out for football next fall instead. They've got a team in the eighth grade. And you'd better not call me Many Horse any more. Not in front of people, anyway. My name's Johnny. Johnny Chapin."

Eighteen

"This is a heck of a way to spend our last day in camp," complained Ed bitterly. "No field trip. No swimming. Nothing but KP."

"I think we were lucky to get off this easily," said Priscilla, shivering a little. "They could have said we could never come back to camp again. Not next year, or ever."

"Maybe that's coming next," said Ed grimly. "Maybe they just haven't got around to that yet. Remember what they said the first day, that people who break rules aren't ever allowed to come back."

"Oh, I hope not," said Priscilla quickly. "Because I want to come back."

"Well, if you do, don't you ever start off by

yourself again," Ed told her grimly. "You're what got me into trouble."

"But I got you out," Johnny Chapin reminded him. "Me and Lightning Bolt. And we wouldn't have been there if we hadn't been friends of Priscilla's."

Ed looked at Johnny to see if he was kidding. He wasn't at all. His sunburned face washed clean of the red and black markings, which he now admitted were borrowed lipstick and eyebrow pencil, was perfectly serious. He was quite a boy, Johnny Chapin, even though he was a little touched on the subject of Indians. And he didn't seem at all embarrassed about being friends with a girl.

"You rescued her, too," Ed reminded him. "The day she wandered off and got lost."

"Oh, that was okay," said Johnny. "It was nice to have somebody to talk to. I was getting tired of having nobody to talk to but Lightning Bolt."

"And he's stopped people from calling you Tex," pointed out Priscilla. "Will you ever forget their faces when the three of us walked up to the fire last night and they found out Johnny had been living around here spying on us for two weeks?"

"I wasn't spying," objected Johnny indignantly. "I was just keeping an eye on things."

"And when they found out it was you who swiped my sleeping bag!" laughed Ed. "I can hardly wait to see the sheriff's face when he gets here. He was so sure it was a tramp."

"I didn't swipe it. I just borrowed it. I was going to return it," frowned Johnny. Then he shook his head ruefully. "*I* can wait to see the sheriff, though. Because he'll have phoned my dad. And Dad will have to haul a horse carrier for Lightning Bolt over here. And he'll be mad anyway. Brother, will I catch it!"

"Why did you run away from home, Johnny?" asked Priscilla, smiling to herself. Johnny's appearance at the campfire last night had solved a problem for her too. Ginny now understood why Tufty couldn't be given the jam sandwich, and the two girls were once more best friends.

"I didn't, really," he explained carefully. "It was just a little vacation. Mom and Dad went on one, and I was expected to go visit my grandmother at Pendleton. Only I didn't mail the letter telling her I was coming. I decided I'd go out and see how my great-great-great-grandfather, Chief Many Horse, got along. The hired hands thought I'd got on the bus that day, only I didn't. I went out to pasture and roped old Lightning Bolt. Red, my own horse, had a lame foot, so I couldn't take him. Then I just started out. I don't see what all the fuss is about. I wasn't lost. I knew where I was all the time."

"You had me fooled," admitted Priscilla. "I

thought you really were an Indian. Were all those stories you told me handed down by your great-great-great-grandfather?"

"No. There haven't been any Tyighs around here for years and years," said Johnny sadly. "I guess everybody but me has just about forgotten there were any. I read all that stuff in books. But it sure sounded good, didn't it?"

"How about that piece of obsidian?" demanded Ed curiously. "Where did you get that?"

"Down in southern Oregon. I was on a trip there with my folks last summer," said Johnny. "I was going to try to make some arrowheads like those I already have. I bought them in a store that sells Indian stuff in Pendleton. Cost me seventy-five cents apiece. That's highway robbery, so I figured I'd make my own. Only I didn't have the knack."

"We could do it in the workshop," suggested Ed. "We've got the things to work with there."

Johnny got to his feet, his eyes brightening.

"Show me," he demanded.

Ed led the way and pulled back the tent flap with a flourish. All the campers were proud of the workshop. There was a diamond saw, as well as polishing wheels. There was all the necessary equipment for testing rocks and minerals, and there were the specimens the campers themselves had collected. Anyone could pack his discoveries away in his own tent, of course, but it was more fun to leave them out on display until the last minute before departure, so that the others could admire and compare.

Johnny was properly impressed by the wheels and the saw, particularly when diamond dust was explained to him, but he lifted his eyebrows at the specimen table.

"What good are they?" he demanded. "Just rocks, with one side polished up."

"But they aren't all rocks," cried Priscilla quickly. "Most of them are minerals."

"Minerals, rocks, what's the difference?" insisted Johnny. "They're just stuff lying around that you picked up and dragged in. They're not good for anything."

He winked at her and shrugged his shoulders

Priscilla's mouth opened to take up the argument, then she caught her cousin's eye. He winked at her and shrugged his shoulders. Some people just had to learn about such things the hard way.

"I guess they aren't good for much," admitted Priscilla meekly, "unless you happen to be a rock hound. The way we are."